His body burned up with desire.

They just had to get through this before Ash gave into his baser instincts and, for the first time in his career on an active tour of duty, mixed his army life with his personal one.

Every time he thought he was back in control, Fliss slipped beneath the surface and unraveled him like a kitten would toy with a ball of yarn. Suddenly, he didn't want to fight it anymore. He wanted to know how it would feel to give in—just this once—and steal one perfect kiss from those plump, quivering lips.

One kiss.

No, he'd survived ambushes, engaged in fifty-hour firefights and fought with the enemy in hand-to-hand combat. He'd pick any one of those over letting this woman get close enough to sneak behind his armor.

Just one kiss.

It was a constant battle between his baser instincts and his brain. *Only an animal couldn't control their baser instincts*, he warned himself contemptuously. Besides, this woman could hurt him more than any enemy could.

But just one kiss.

Dear Reader,

This is my first story set in and around the fictional Military Camp Razorwire, set in the middle of nowhere, thousands of miles from home—and I'm enjoying writing several more.

I am a great supporter of our armed forces and am often humbled by the heroic stories of soldiers, both from history and present day, male and female, who have made that split-second decision to put someone else's life ahead of their own, and then dismiss it as *"something anyone else would have done."*

Both my hero, a dedicated infantry soldier, and my heroine, an army trauma doctor on the helicopter emergency response, are dedicated to their careers because both are trying to make up for unhappy childhoods, if for different reasons. Working together proves a distraction neither of them appreciate, yet ultimately neither of them can hold out.

I have great fun writing about the push and pull of heroes and heroines who are committed to their careers only to meet—and strive in vain to resist— the one person who can get under their skin. The one person who can make them forget everything they had hitherto held important.

I do so hope you enjoy reading Fliss and Ash's story as much as I did writing it.

Charlotte x

ENCOUNTER WITH A COMMANDING OFFICER

———

CHARLOTTE HAWKES

❖HARLEQUIN® MEDICAL ROMANCE™

Recycling programs
for this product may
not exist in your area.

ISBN-13: 978-0-373-21548-5

Encounter with a Commanding Officer

First North American Publication 2017

Copyright © 2017 by Charlotte Hawkes

Printed in U.S.A.

Books by Charlotte Hawkes

Harlequin Medical Romance

The Army Doc's Secret Wife
The Surgeon's Baby Surprise

Visit the Author Profile page
at Harlequin.com for more titles.

To Flo,
Thank you for all your understanding
and patience this past difficult year.
x

**Praise for
Charlotte Hawkes**

"Well-written, well thought out and one of
greatness.... Definitely one to pick up for an
amazing story."

—*Harlequin Junkie* on
The Surgeon's Baby Surprise

CHAPTER ONE

'So, I TAKE it you've never had the pleasure of meeting Colonel Man Candy either?'

Fliss paused in her half-hearted attempt to cut up her breakfast with the flimsy plastic knife and fork, and stared at her friend incredulously. Then, given the din of the several hundred men in the Army mess tent, assumed she must have misheard. Clearly the latest forty-eight-hour shift had messed with her imagination.

'Say again? For a minute there I thought you said Colonel Man Candy.'

'Yeah, I did.' Her friend grinned wickedly. 'But it gets better. Apparently up until a few months ago he was Major Man Candy.'

Fliss snorted. '*Major* Man Candy? Seriously, Elle?'

'Seriously.'

'People *actually* call him that?'

'They actually do.' Her friend shrugged. 'To the extent that I have no idea what his real name is. But I *can* tell you that a good portion of the camp is buzzing about his arrival, male and female as it happens, though for different reasons. Apparently, he's also something of a maverick who has risked his life for his men on multiple occasions.'

Unconvinced, Fliss wrinkled her nose.

'I haven't heard any *buzz*. Not even a single *z*.'

'No, well, you wouldn't—you don't indulge in gossip and anyone who knows you knows better than to engage with you unless it's strictly Army related, preferably medical.'

'I do…gossip.' Fliss nodded uncertainly, biting back the fact she'd been about to comment that it would be inappropriate for any colonel, Man Candy or otherwise, to have any kind of relationship with most of the camp.

Her friend's snort said it all.

'Fliss, you *cannot* gossip for the life of you. And certainly not about fellow military colleagues.'

'I don't agree. For a start *this,* what we're doing right now, is gossip.'

'No, this is *me* gossiping and *you* listening, about to say something like, *Well, interpersonal relationships between ranks aren't appropriate because they compromise the integrity of a unit.'*

Caught red-handed, Fliss could only flush as her friend laughed fondly. She lifted her head.

'Well…it *is* true.'

'Fliss, you know that I love you. In fact, if you were a stick of rock you'd have *Army Rules and Regulations* stamped through and through.'

Fliss blew out a deep breath, a familiar ripple of uncertainty and frustration lapping somewhere inside her before settling back down again. She'd always been known as *serious* Fliss, *nerdy* Fliss, *prim and proper* Fliss; she couldn't help it, it was ingrained in her. The result, no doubt, of having being raised from the age of eight by an uncle who was a military man through and through, believing in the extremely high reputation of the British Army with its strong sense of discipline, values and ethics.

And he'd drilled it into her. Not that she was complaining—her highly principled uncle had been her one saviour, her rock, throughout her life. The one person who hadn't seen her as a burden, but as a bright though shy girl with potential. The one person who hadn't rejected her. Her uncle had spent twenty-five years supporting her and encouraging her. He'd been so proud of her when she'd finally achieved her dream of becoming an Army trauma doctor, just as she was immensely proud that he was now one of the most highly decorated generals in the army, and that she could call herself his niece.

Spearing a lump of scrambled egg, Fliss

popped it into her mouth, but her throat was a little too tight to swallow. Not for the first time, she wished she could forget the baggage and lessons of her past. Just once it would be nice to know what it felt like not to be the solid, dependable Fliss who immediately assessed the ramifications of any given situation, but to be more like her friend, Elle, who was always able to have a carefree laugh and whose sunny disposition and kind-hearted openness made her popular wherever she went.

'Go on, then—' Fliss plastered a cheery smile onto her face '—tell me more about Major Man Candy.'

She didn't miss the flash of suspicion on her friend's face but, to her credit, Elle didn't question it.

'Okay, so it seems he's been infantry major on the front line in warzones, doing several back-to-back tours of duty over the last few years, and, like I said, he has a reputation as being quite the maverick, the kind of guy they make Hollywood films about. Plus, Man Candy has the kind of military commendation record which would leave even the most decorated generals or admirals envious.'

'And now he's a colonel in a non-combat zone?' Fliss looked dubious. 'Stuck within the confines of a place like Camp Razorwire and meant to work behind a desk all day instead of out in the field. He isn't going to like that, is he?'

She could still remember the year when her uncle had been promoted from a field-based officer to one who spent most of his time in barracks. He'd found the transition hard and Fliss had hated to see his frustration.

'Well, if half the single female contingent I've heard chatting about him get their way, I think he's going to be too busy dealing with ambushes and bombardments of a more sexual nature to miss being on the front line in the middle of the action.'

'You make it seem like they're all highly sex-charged.' Fliss frowned, aware she was being prudish but unable to help herself. 'They *are* professional soldiers.'

'And they're also women,' Elle pointed out airily, accustomed to Fliss's more steadfast opinions. '*Single* women. Out here for six months at a time. They're entitled to a bit of harmless flirtation in their downtime.'

'Until it all goes wrong,' Fliss shot back, but a hint of niggling doubt had already set in. Elle's argument was all starting to sound a little too pointed.

'For example, if two officers—let's say like you and oh, I don't know, a certain new colonel—were to… As long as you were discreet, what harm could it cause?'

'I knew it,' exclaimed Fliss, dropping her plastic cutlery on the paper plate. 'Forget it, Elle. That's just not my style.'

'Why not? Because you've never done it before? So what? Maybe this is your one time to do something crazy. Especially now that idiot ex of yours is out of the picture.'

A heaviness pressed on Fliss's chest. Not sadness exactly, but a sense of…failure. She strived to ignore it.

'Because he doesn't sound like the kind of guy I'd go for. And please don't mention Robert—you were always more than honest with me about your feelings about him.'

'All right.' Elle chuckled fondly. 'But, from what I've heard, Man Candy is everyone's type.'

'He doesn't sound like mine.'

In fact, he sounded the complete opposite. Robert had been solid, steady, dependable. The pressure increased on her chest. She'd been attracted to the fact that, like her, he was dedicated to his career, driven to achieve. She'd thought they were a perfect match. A logical couple. A practical choice.

Look where that had got her.

'Well, if anyone would be immune to the Man Candy Effect it would be you,' Elle teased, oblivious. 'You're probably the most highly principled person even *I* know.'

'Yeah, yeah, Fusty Fliss.' The old nickname slipped out before Fliss had time to think about it. 'I remember.'

'Where did *that* come from?' Elle exclaimed, setting her plastic cutlery down in surprise. 'I haven't heard anyone call you that since first year of uni.'

Colour heated Fliss's cheeks. She hadn't meant for Elle to realise she'd been feeling a little vulnerable lately. It was a weakness Fliss wasn't proud of, and didn't want to reveal. Even to her best friend.

'Brody Gordon,' Fliss mumbled. 'And you're right, the guy was an idiot. I don't know why I even said it. Just forget it, okay?'

Ducking her head, she resumed her breakfast but her appetite was waning. She might have known her friend wouldn't let it drop.

'Is this about Buttoned-Down Bob?' Elle demanded. Too close to the bone for Fliss's liking.

'Don't call him that.' She kept her voice soft, trying to play the topic down. But Elle was like the proverbial dog once it had a juicy bone in its sights. 'He's a respected surgeon. A good man.'

Elle wasn't having any of it.

'He's also as boring as they come. Everything he did was so painfully predictable.'

'Breaking up with me via a *Dear John* letter whilst I was stuck out here, at Camp Razorwire, in the middle of vast nothingness was hardly predictable,' Fliss pointed out.

'All right, but, that aside, he was so numbingly characterless. And, before you tell me I'm wrong, tell me that losing him has broken your heart.'

A restlessness rolled around her chest, along with something else when she thought about Robert—something she didn't want to identify.

'Don't be so melodramatic.'

'You're side-stepping,' Elle said, not unkindly. 'Tell me your heart broke when you read his words. Tell me you rushed to the phone to find some way to communicate with him and find out what went wrong.'

'You know I didn't,' Fliss muttered, the restless rolling increasing like the rumble of thunder before a flash of lightning.

'Then tell me you love him, you miss him, you don't know how you're going to get by without him.'

She knew what Elle was trying to say but it wasn't as simple as that.

'Just because I'm not racked with despair doesn't mean I didn't love Robert in my own way. It doesn't mean I wasn't hurt.'

Yet she couldn't explain it to her friend. No,

theirs hadn't been a great romance like Elle had with her own fiancé and childhood sweetheart, but it had been comfortable. He hadn't looked at her with shame like her grandparents had, and he'd never raged at her like her mother had. Life with him *had* been predictable, yes. But Fliss had appreciated that. She'd thought they both had.

It had hurt to read his letter and find out that even Robert needed more from a relationship, to see in black and white that even *he* found her too emotionally distant. The worst of it was that she knew he was right. The heaviness in her chest felt like a rising reservoir of water, its swirling dark depths drawing her closer to the edge. She'd chosen Robert because she'd thought they had the same life goals, and because she'd thought she couldn't be hurt. But his letter had felt like a painful echo of her childhood rejection.

'I did care for Robert,' she told her friend quietly. 'But I was never *in love* with him. It isn't his fault that I couldn't give him more. It's mine. I don't have that capacity in me, Elle. I don't do passion and emotion and intense love.'

'Bull,' Elle snorted. 'You just haven't met the right guy. Trust me, when you do, you'll forget all these daft rules and fears of yours. When you find *the one*, you'll know it.'

'Like you and Stevie?' Fliss said softly.

A shadow skittered unexpectedly over her best friend's face and Elle suddenly looked a million miles away—or, more likely, three thousand miles. Concern flooded through Fliss as she placed her hand on her friend's to draw Elle's focus.

'Elle, is everything okay?'

Elle blinked, the instantly over-bright smile not fooling Fliss at all.

'Of course I am. I'm just trying to help you move on from Buttoned— Sorry, Robert. And maybe have a bit of fun in the process. And, since Man Candy is off-limits to me, I have to live vicariously through you.'

Fliss bit back the questions tumbling around her head. The Army dining hall was hardly the best place to grill her best friend but she knew she had to talk to Elle the first chance they got.

'Just promise me you'll think about it? One crazy fling. There's no better time than now and, by the sounds of it, there's no better choice than Man Candy.'

'You realise, of course, that even if I did fall over on my way out of here today, bump my head, change my personality and decide that hot sex is indeed going to sort out all my problems, then there's still the issue that he's an infantry colonel and therefore nothing to do with our medical unit and, with around eight thousand of us out here in Razorwire, we're hardly likely to cross paths.'

'So, you are at least open to the mere possibility of it?'

Fliss rolled her eyes.

'If that's what you want to take from what I said, then fine.'

'Good.' Elle nodded, swiping half a round of uneaten toast from Fliss's plate. 'By the way, did I mention that Simon wants to see you for an oh-eight-hundred briefing?'

Fliss groaned. Colonel Simon Johnson was the Commanding Officer of their medical unit. A brilliant surgeon and, like a high proportion of the medical team, a civilian volunteer. This was his second tour to Razorwire and Fliss both respected and liked him, but right now, after a forty-eight-hour shift, all she'd been looking forward to was eating her scram and then heading for the Army cot-bed which was calling to her from the shipping container she and Elle shared.

It was because of her tiredness that it took her a moment too long to register Elle's affected air of innocence.

'Wait, I have a briefing? What for?'

'Hmm? Oh, the new infantry Commanding Officer replacing Colonel Waterson is arriving.'

'Ah.'

Both women fell into a few seconds of respectful silence. They'd only met him once, but Colonel Waterson's death had been a shock. Razorwire was in a non-combat environment, its task to help local communities rebuild and improve. But the former infantry colonel hadn't been content to stay behind a desk and had flown out, on a spurious task, to a danger zone some six hundred miles away. His death had knocked the rest of the camp, not to mention rocked his own unit who were now being dragged into an internal investigation which, though standard, had the effect of further dragging down their already low morale.

Fliss could only hope that the arrival of their new Commanding Officer would help the infantry unit to heal. Not least because that particular infantry unit provided the protection units, or Quick Reaction Forces, for any other teams travelling outside of the camp, from logistics to her own medical team.

'Anyway—' Elle broke the silence firmly, both women knowing that, especially out here, far from home, it didn't pay to dwell '—since the new colonel's men form the four-man QRF teams we work with on a daily basis, Simon felt we should meet him.'

Fliss narrowed her eyes at her friend. She

should have seen the set-up coming from the start.

'And this CO, is he by any chance the all-singing, all-dancing Colonel *Man Candy*?'

'Why, now you mention it—' grinned Elle '—I do believe he is. Though I think you should wait for Simon to introduce you. I don't know how the new colonel would react to you actually calling him *Man Candy* to his face.'

Fliss could only shake her head as her friend chortled with laughter. At the end of the day, she reasoned to herself, it was only a bit of fun between two friends. Man Candy was hardly going to make her go weak at the knees. The things she'd heard other women talk about had never happened to her; it just wasn't who she was.

'You're a sneaky sod, do you know that? And anyway, if you really think someone who's as allegedly dynamic as Man Candy is going to fall for an uptight wallflower like me, then maybe you're the one who took a knock on the head.'

'Piffle,' Elle sputtered.

'Piffle?'

'You heard. You've never appreciated how attractive you are; everywhere you go there are guys just clamouring for attention but you never notice. You're intelligent and wittier than you give yourself credit for, and definitely not a wallflower.'

Gratitude bloomed in Fliss like a thousand flowers suddenly opening their petals. What would she do without her uncle or Elle? They were the only two people she would ever trust. The only two people to whom she mattered. She didn't need men like Robert; they didn't offer her anything more than she already had.

'You're a good friend, Elle,' Fliss said, suddenly serious.

'That is true.' Elle consulted her chunky sports watch. 'You'd better go; briefing is in ten. Don't forget what I said. Open mind, yes? What harm can it do?'

'Fine.' Fliss shoved her chair back and stood up, lodging an apple between her teeth as she picked up her tray to take to the clearing section. 'But don't hold your breath.'

Man Candy or not, she was never going to believe in love at first sight. It just wasn't who she was.

'Ah, you're here.' The medical Commanding Officer beamed with something approaching relief as Fliss was ushered in by the adjutant.

By the look on Simon's face, the new colonel wasn't quite as sweet as his nickname suggested. Stepping into the office, she turned to greet the new infantry colonel for the first time.

It was as if time caught a breath; everything

happened in slow motion. Even the air felt as thick and sticky as the sweet honey she'd spread over her toast at breakfast. All Fliss could do was suck in a long breath and stare, her mind suddenly empty of anything but the man standing, *dominating* the space.

So this was Colonel Man Candy?

The nickname simply didn't do him justice. It suggested sugar-coated and frivolous. This man was anything but.

He was tall, powerful and all hard edges more lethal than a bayonet on the end of a rifle. His uniform—sharp and crisp with that edge to it that seemed to mark infantrymen out over all other soldiers—did little to conceal the physique beneath. If anything, it enhanced it. The perfectly folded up shirtsleeves which clung lovingly to impressive biceps revealed equally strong, tanned forearms. But it wasn't merely his forearms, more something about his demeanour which suggested to Fliss that he was a soldier who was used to physical exertion in the field. Certainly not the kind of man to relish being stuck behind a desk. He exuded a commanding air. Rough. Dangerous.

He was definitely more suited to an adrenalin-fuelled life on the front line than being stuck here in the safe confines of a place like Razorwire.

Abruptly, Fliss realised that even as she was assessing the Colonel, he was appraising her too. Narrowed eyes, the colour of mountain shale and just as inhospitable, slid over her. And everywhere they travelled, they left a scorching sensation on her skin. She wanted to move, to say something. Instead she stood rooted to the spot, her throat tight and her heart pounding out a military tattoo in her chest.

Something unfurled in the pit of Fliss's stomach. Something which she didn't recognise at all but which made her feel the need to regroup. Something which scared her, yet was also perhaps a little thrilling. And then it was gone, so fast that she wondered if she hadn't simply imagined it.

Slowly, she became aware of Simon speaking with a forced cheerfulness, as though he could sense the undertones but couldn't compute them.

'Colonel, this is Major Felicity Delaunay, the trauma doctor who leads one of our primary MERT crews,' Simon introduced her, referring to the Medical Emergency Response Team which flew out from the camp in helicopters to retrieve casualties from outside the wire.

'Major, let me introduce Colonel Asher Stirling, the new CO replacing the late Colonel Waterson.'

'Colonel,' Fliss choked out, finally finding her voice as she proffered her hand, relieved to see that it wasn't shaking.

The new Colonel didn't take it. Instead, he folded his arms across his chest in a very deliberate move.

'Major Delaunay,' he bit out. 'So you're the doc who thinks she's so important she's risking the safety of my men, not to mention the rest of her own crew.'

His hostile glower pinned her in place. She wanted to snatch her own gaze away but found she couldn't. He was too mesmerising.

Still, a defiant flame flickered into life inside her.

'Would you care to elaborate, *sir*?'

She made a point of emphasising the acknowledgement of his superior rank. She didn't like what he was suggesting, but she had no intention of being accused of insubordination as well.

'I'm saying your position is on the helicopter, receiving incoming casualties and staying where my men can protect you.'

His voice was deep, his tone peremptory. And Fliss didn't just hear the words, she *felt* them too. Compression waves coursed through her whole being. He didn't just have the rank of a colonel, he *oozed* it. Authoritative and all-consuming. She had never reacted so innately to anyone—to any *man*—before. She hadn't even known it was possible to do so.

She was vaguely aware of Simon attempting to interject but it felt as though there were only the two of them in the room. The CO soon faded out, making some spurious excuse and dashing for the door.

'Is this about the incident last week when I had to leave the heli to attend a casualty?'

'As I understand it, not just last week, no,' the new Colonel continued coldly. 'My men are there to protect you…'

'They're there to protect the helicopter, the asset,' she cut in.

Waves of tightly controlled fury bounced off him.

'They are *tasked* to protect you, but I understand you make that impossible for them on a regular basis. Yet if anything were to happen to you, my men would be responsible.'

'Your *men*…'

She stopped and bit her lip, her sense of self-preservation finally kicking in. He clearly only had half the story and if he thought she was just going to stand there without setting the record straight then he could think again. But as much as this dressing-down galled her, she refused to speak badly of his men. They'd been through enough.

Straightening her spine, she jutted her chin out to give the impression she wasn't intimidated. Instead, it only reminded her just how close to each other they were standing. White heat snaked through her. She had a feeling that when this man spoke, people listened. But Fliss forced herself to push it to the side, forced herself to wonder if he was equally capable of listening.

She was about to find out.

'Your men are feeling understandably uptight right now, and I appreciate that you're only looking out for your new unit, but there *are* two sides to this story, Colonel.'

'And you're about to enlighten me?'

It was phrased as a question but the gravelly sound resonated through her, pulling her stomach impossibly taut. *This was it*. She'd challenged him and now she was going to have to back it up. Either that, or he would dismiss her as weak for ever.

She gritted her teeth but refused to back down. That wasn't what her uncle had ever taught her. And, besides, a terrible part of her desperately wanted this man's respect. His esteem.

'I understand that you've recently been promoted to colonel, and that you were a major on the front line before that, so this is a new unit for you, and these are men that you don't know well yet. I appreciate that you're only looking out for them after what happened with Colonel Waterson. He was *their* CO and it was a shock to them. But it was a shock to us all. Razorwire isn't in a warzone; we have a different mission to whatever we've had before. Whatever *you've* had before, on the front line.'

'And your point, Major?' he demanded impatiently.

'My point, Colonel, is that your men— *my* QRF—are jumpy at the moment. I know why—a helicopter is a big target for anyone on the ground with rocket launchers, and the QRF don't want us to hang around too long. But we're not in a warzone, Colonel. We're on a Hearts and Minds mission and I think your men have forgotten that in the wake of Colonel Waterson's death. They never had a problem with my getting off the heli before, and they won't again in a few weeks. And the reason I jump off is because the casualties who can't get to the heli in time might not make it if we just abandon them.'

There it was, she noted triumphantly.

The flash in his eyes suggested her words had hit home. She'd suspected that, of all people, this new Colonel wasn't the type to leave a fallen man behind. And she was right; he'd reacted as soon as she'd said the word *abandon.*

Still, he clearly wasn't about to give in that easily. And that didn't surprise her.

'My men informed me that the casualties weren't in immediate danger.'

'With all due respect, sir, your men aren't trauma doctors. I am. Just because there are no bombs out here, no IEDs, with fatalities and casualties requiring multiple amputations, doesn't mean there aren't urgent cases.'

'I am well aware of that, Major,' he ground out, his eyes drilling into her. 'I've carried a fair few men to a MERT over the years.'

'Yes, but usually from the front line, I understand. Out here, we have non-combat injuries to deal with, from Road Traffic Accidents to local kids in gas bottle explosions around their home, from peace-keeping troops with appendicitis to local women in labour requiring emergency medical intervention. It might not always look fatal to your battle-hardened troops but fatality comes in less obvious guises. And I made a judgement call each time.'

And she'd been right each time too, not that she was about to offer that information up. It would have far greater impact when the Colonel found that out for himself. And she knew without a doubt that he would.

'Indeed?' The Colonel raised his eyebrows at her.

His mind was not entirely swayed but he was clearly considering her position. She suppressed a thrill of pleasure. It was a victory of sorts. And all the sweeter because, for a second there, she'd almost lost herself to a side of her character she had never before known existed. A side which wasn't immune—as she had so long believed—to the tedious and feeble vagaries of an instant physical attraction.

But she had fought it, and she had won. Hopefully she'd managed to convince the new Colonel to get his men to back off for the last few weeks of her tour of duty and, with him being infantry and her being medical, there was no reason she'd have to see him again.

Relief mingled with something else which Fliss didn't care to identify.

It was all short-lived.

He stepped in closer, almost menacingly so, and instinctively her eyes widened a fraction, her breath growing shallower.

He picked up on it immediately, but it was only when his eyes dropped instantly to her rapidly rising and falling chest, his nostrils flaring as she heard his sharp intake of breath, that Fliss realised he was as affected by her as she was by him.

Her? The girl Brody Gordon had referred to as Fusty Fliss? Attracting a guy as utterly masculine as the Colonel? It hardly seemed possible.

And then she realised what this uncharacteristic moment of weakness was all about for her. It wasn't some incredible, irresistible attraction at all. It was merely the fact that Robert's rejection had exposed unhealed wounds from her past which she had scarcely buried beneath the surface. Old rejections and feelings of inadequacy that her mother, her grandparents and boys like Brody Gordon had cruelly instigated.

She wanted to pull away from the Colonel now, use the revelation to her advantage. But it seemed that even knowing the truth wasn't helping her to resist him. He pinned her down, his eyes locked with hers, inching forward until they were toe to toe and her head was tilted right up to hold the stare. For several long seconds Fliss was sure she stopped breathing.

And then, finally, he broke the spell.

'I must say, *Major*, my interest is piqued.' The fierce expression had lifted from his rough-hewn face to be replaced by a look which was simultaneously wicked and challenging. White heat licked low in her belly.

'I understand your next forty-eight-hour shift begins at oh-six-hundred tomorrow?'

'That's right,' she acknowledged carefully, a sense of foreboding brewing in the tiny office.

'Good. Then I'll accompany you for the first twenty-four hours and we'll see what we discover, shall we?'

Her whole body shivered.

'You can't do that; you don't have the authority. You're not my commanding officer. You're not even medical.'

'No—' he seemed unfazed '—but I *am* the CO of the infantry unit which provides your protection unit and, since they are my guys, I *do* have a reason to be on that heli. I hardly think your buddy Simon is going to object when I run it by him. Do you?'

'It's *my* heli, *my* run. I could tell my CO it wouldn't be appropriate.'

She was grasping at straws and they both knew it. The wicked smile cranked up a notch, and so did the fire burning low in her core. He dropped his voice to a husky rasp which seemed to graze her body as surely as if he'd run callused fingers over the sensitive skin of her belly.

'And on what grounds exactly are you going to object?'

He had a point; she could hardly tell Simon that she didn't want to be in close confinement on a heli with the new infantry CO because there was an inexplicable chemistry between them that, when she was around him, made her body heat up and her brain shut down.

She was trapped and they both knew it. Worse, Fliss was left with the distinct impression that a tiny part of her actually *liked* it.

Clenching her fists and spinning around as Simon finally bustled back into the room, Fliss studiously ignored the terrifying voice which whispered that the truth was, she just might have experienced her very first *lust* at first sight.

CHAPTER TWO

CROUCHED IN THE corner of the cramped, swelter-
ing, noisy Chinook—kitted out as a full airborne
emergency room, its engines the only thing one
could smell or hear—Ash fought down the nausea which was threatening to overwhelm him.

He'd seen the MERT in action too many times
to count during his seven tours of duty over the
last decade, several back to back. He had an incredible respect for the doctors and medics who
ran what was, essentially, an airborne operating room. Many of his men, his *friends*, were
still alive today because of the swift, skilled ac-
tions of MERT teams. But although he'd carried many casualties to the heli as part of the
infantry team on the ground, the only time he'd
actually been on board had been when he himself had been seriously injured.

Ash kept his eyes firmly open. If he closed
them, the sounds were too brutally familiar.
If he closed them, the scents, the turbulence,
transported him right back to that day. If he

closed them, he could almost feeling his life ebbing away.

Instead, he studiously watched the attractive blonde major who was running this flying operating room with impressive command and focus. Even now she was diligently prepping any last pieces of equipment. He could imagine her as the focused, methodical doctor, but he still couldn't imagine her ever breaking the rules to save a soldier, the way his new unit had claimed she'd done on more than one occasion.

But that wasn't the reason he was here, was it?

From the minute she'd walked into that room yesterday, she'd somehow slipped under his skin and he'd found himself reacting to her in a way that made him feel out of control. And for Ash it was all about being in control. About not allowing himself to feel. Because feeling meant being at the mercy of emotions. And that wasn't something he permitted.

He'd kept an iron grip on his emotions for two decades now. They were a liability he couldn't afford. Not since the beatings, the push and pull from the miserable care home to the squalor of foster homes, to his dad, who'd somehow convinced the authorities he'd stopped the drinking, right up until the cycle had started all over again. Only Rosie and Wilf had shown him another way. They'd been the only foster parents able to take on that angry, out-of-control kid that he'd been and show him love, and hope, and a way out.

A darkness unfurled in him, snaking its devious way up to constrict his chest painfully until he found it hard even to breathe. Controlling his emotions, keeping people at arm's length, had been an important lesson growing up and it was even more important now. Out here on a tour of duty and waiting, at any time, for a phone call to tell him the inevitable had happened, that Rosie had finally lost her fight and he would have to fly home for what was likely to be the worst funeral of his life.

Perhaps it was no wonder, then, that he'd reacted as he had done when the Major had strode into that office yesterday. Even now, at the mere memory, awareness crackled through his body, dancing over the darkness which had filled him a moment ago as though it was nothing. As though that forbidding fear couldn't compete with the light-hearted lust which toyed playfully with him. As though it knew that once, *just this once,* he could be tempted to cross the line and consider a hot…fling with someone like the Major, just because it offered him the promise of distraction, a release from the tension of waiting. Of not knowing.

That's not going to happen.

Furiously, he shoved the idea aside. He *never* mixed personal relationships with his career. Not out here. Not within the Army. It had too much potential to become...messy.

Yet his eyes slid inexorably across the heli to the commanding Major. She made him react to her in the basest of ways. Yet she also challenged him mentally. He hadn't intended to give her the dressing-down that he had, anticipating instead that he'd voice his concerns and find out what she had to say before making a judgement. Instead, he'd allowed his attraction to her to override his usual common sense.

But, instead of meekly surrendering, she'd looked him in the eye and refuted every one of his statements clearly and confidently. And that had piqued an interest in Ash. Before he'd known where he was, he'd bagged himself a ringside seat to all the shouts her MERT would respond to over the next twenty-four hours.

This wasn't helping.

He dragged his attention away from her and concentrated on the four-man QRF team made up from his new infantry unit. The Major had been right about them too. It hadn't taken him long yesterday to find out that his new unit *was* particularly wound up about the incident which had claimed the life of Colonel Waterson. He would do well to boost their morale and he had no doubt that, given half a chance, the Major would happily instruct him on that too.

And now he was back to her. Again.

But now, for the first time he could ever recall, his iron grip, honed over the last two decades, was slipping. His focus threatened. And all because of this one woman.

His gaze slipped back to the by-the-book Major as he tried to work out what was so different about her. So prim and proper, she was certainly attractive with those barbed Nordic blue eyes and blonde hair pulled into such an eye-wateringly severe yet generous bun that his fingers had actually itched to reach up and release. To slide his fingers through the silk curtain and soften the strait-laced doctor, even a fraction.

What the heck was wrong with him?

It was the last thing Ash needed. Not just because she was General Delaunay's niece but because this was the first role Ash had taken behind the wire, in the relative safety of Camp Razorwire. He certainly felt on edge at the prospect of facing the next few years behind a desk instead of out in the field. Out where he belonged. Barely a month ago he'd been a major himself, on the front line and leading his company as he risked his own life alongside his men. Now he was a colonel, in charge of a battalion and destined—maybe not on this tour of duty, but on a future one—not to lead his men but to *send* them into potential danger zones.

How the hell was he supposed to get used to that?

Behind a desk wasn't where he functioned best. All his career he had experienced the adrenalin kick, the fear, the buzz, and he'd been in control.

Now, as galling as it was to admit, he felt lost.

Suddenly, the heli filled with dust as it dropped, the rotor blades churning up the ground covering and drawing it into the back on the air currents, blinding them all. Ash buried his nose into his combat jacket like a filter so that he could breathe. And then they landed, rough and abrupt, and the dust was sucked quickly instantly out, leaving the aircraft clear again.

It took everything Ash had to fight his instinct to jump out of the back ahead of his QRF to help secure the area around the heli, safe zone or not. As two of his men secured the rear, where soldiers were already running across the open ground carrying a litter-bound casualty, the other two men leapt up to man the ramp-mounted and side-mounted machine guns respectively. They were smooth and slick and

Ash nodded to himself in satisfaction. It was what he'd expected, but still, it was good to see.

'RTA on the Main Supply Route,' the young team medic for the soldiers' unit rushed ahead to the heli to brief the MERT, yelling over the din. 'Local guy driving a flatbed truck across the bridge running perpendicular above us when he suffered a tyre blow out and lost control. Nothing he could do, his truck jack-knifed and he crashed through the barrier and landed on our convoy. We've got three casualties.'

Even as he finished, the soldiers had already reached them with the first casualty and the Major and her team efficiently hauled the litter on board and began their medical care. Just behind, two soldiers were helping the injured local man to hobble to the heli, an open fracture to one arm and clearly shaken. Walking wounded, that was always preferable. The teams would settle him in a seat and then pass him on to the camp hospital for care. But, even from across the helicopter, Ash could see that the first victim had significant crush injuries. He wasn't a doctor but Ash had enough experience to know. All vital signs were absent and, to all intents and purposes, the soldier was gone. But it wasn't the MERT's place to call time of death; they didn't have the authority. That could only be done when they returned to Camp Razorwire and a team from the hospital came out.

Not that you'd know it from the Major's poker face; there was no sign of defeat in her expression, nothing to knock the morale of the soldiers on the ground, who wanted her to save the life of their buddy. Instead the MERT were doing their job and starting care, the Major already checking the casualty's airway and giving oxygen as the team began cardiopulmonary resuscitation. It meant a lot out here, in the middle of vast nothingness. Back on the front line, it would have been exactly the kind of mental boost the guys would need. A reluctant admiration sparked in Ash.

Suddenly, a movement in his peripheral caught Ash's attention. A third team carrying a casualty, stretcher-bound like the first, was rounding the bend approximately one hundred metres away. Even from that distance there was evidence of heavy blood loss but what worried Ash more was the long metal rod protruding from the casualty's abdomen. There was no way they would be able to get the soldier onto the heli like that.

In an instant, Ash had sprung out from his corner and jumped off the ramp to dart, body low against the downdraught of the rotors, across the open ground. There was definitely a sandstorm coming in; he'd spent enough time out in the field to be able to sense it before almost anyone else. Reaching the litter, he was relieved to find the casualty on his side, delirious but mercifully still alive.

'Set him down gently, lads,' Ash commanded quietly but firmly enough to counter their resistance out of loyalty to their friend. 'He's not going to get on board like that.'

Ash watched as, for a split second, understandable desperation to get their buddy to the heli warred with following a senior officer's instruction. It was only when he heard the voice over his shoulder that he realised the Major had followed right behind him carrying an emergency kit bag.

'The Colonel's right, lads. I need to check your buddy out first and we'll go from there.'

Pushing briskly through, the Major settled next to the litter and pushed lightly to encourage the soldiers to set it down on the level ground.

'What's his name?' she asked.

'Hollings.'

'Corporal Hollings.'

'Okay—' she nodded, checking the lad's vital signs '—and his first name?'

'Oh, right. It's Andy.'

'Andy, can you hear me? You've got the MERT

here now; we're just going to get you ready for transport, okay?'

Ash watched as she began to administer oxygen, all the while calming the other soldiers and creating some space around them.

'We're going to need to cut the rod down to a more manageable size prior to transport.' She lifted her head to look directly at him. They both knew the MERT wouldn't be able to wait.

Quickly, Ash dropped down until they were close enough to murmur without broadcasting. 'There's a sandstorm coming in.'

'We need to get him out of here as quickly as we can.'

'I'll handle it. How long do you need?'

'Longer than we've got,' she muttered grimly. 'Radial pulse is weak, thready. He's not moving air around and there's pressure in the pleural space. I can carry out a needle decompression but it's only a temporary measure. All the good kit is on the heli. Because of the location of the rod I can't get him into a supine position. And that's without knowing for sure what damage he might have caused internally.'

With a curt nod, Ash raced back to the heli to relay the information, telling them to leave now but to call in the other MERT. At least that way it would have the wait time. The Major had better be able to do what was necessary in that window. Once the storm closed in the helis wouldn't be able to fly and travelling by road would take too long.

He had to admit, though, that he'd seen a lot of good trauma doctors in his time, but the Major had something extra about her, an edge, which he couldn't help but respect.

'Any sheltered locations around here?' Ash demanded as he ran back to the casualty, which the Major had already moved further back in anticipation of the dust cloud the departing helicopter would raise.

'There's a couple of abandoned buildings about half a click away, but they're boarded up. We'll have to bust a way in.'

With any luck the MERT would be back before the sandstorm hit. But if they were unlucky, they were going to need a decent place to wait it out, especially with the casualty.

'Grab any kit we might need and show me,' Ash commanded one of the soldiers.

'Okay, when we cut the rod the vibration could cause more internal damage, so you and you hold it absolutely steady,' she was instructing firmly, calmly, ensuring everyone knew their role whilst still efficiently moving along the task. 'And you cut right here, understand?'

'Ma'am.'

Ash was quickly getting the impression that, once this was all over, he was going to owe the Major something of an apology.

CHAPTER THREE

'MAJOR.' ASH STEPPED to one side in the corridor as the team filed out of the briefing room several hours later. 'A word.'

'Colonel?'

'I wanted to say that was nice work this morning.'

She eyed him carefully, the corners of her mouth twitching before glancing around to ensure everyone had left.

'Is that your idea of an apology?'

She was teasing him?

Something wound around Ash's gut. Hot, raw. It pulled tight.

He fought it. Drew in a sharp breath.

'No, it's my idea of an acknowledgement. If you hadn't leapt off the heli like that, prepared to be left in the middle of nowhere, Corporal Hollings would probably never have made it back here alive. Good work.'

'He also might not have made it if you hadn't secured that compound the way you did. We all played a part in that success,' she breathed.

'Well…' His voice was huskier than usual and Ash consoled himself with the fact that she didn't know him well enough to know that.

He silenced the voice that whispered it was a shame she didn't know him well enough to know that.

'So is that really what you stopped me out here to tell me?'

She held his gaze unwaveringly, drawing him inexorably down into those seductive and all too perceptive depths. He couldn't recall if he'd ever wanted any woman quite as much as he wanted her. He kept trying to tell himself that it was just the shared experience out there which had bonded them in a way which wouldn't otherwise have happened. It was hardly surprising. A few hours in such a hostile environment allowed you to see facets of a person it might otherwise take years to unearth.

He knew it was more than that. The chemistry had been palpable from the moment they'd met. It was what had caused him to react so strongly back in her CO's office. Had he really thought that attacking her the way he had instead of getting her side of the story would prove that he hadn't been standing there imagining what it would be like to have been in that office alone and claimed her as though they were teenagers behind the back of the school gym, instead of professional, responsible army officers?

'I did want to mention it. But no, it isn't all I wanted to say, *Major*.' The emphasis of her rank was more to remind himself than her. 'You were right about the men in my new unit. They are finding it difficult to assimilate replacements and, as you identified, because Camp Razorwire isn't a warzone the previous CO may not have paid enough attention to it.'

The tilt of her head, the light in her expression, even the increased respect in her eyes all played to his basic male pride. Ash knew it yet was powerless against it, the raw sexual appeal too strong.

'I'm glad you can see it too.' She nodded sincerely. 'They're good lads; they just need someone who can talk to them in their language, someone who understands what it's like out there on the front line, someone who can take them in hand.'

It was clear to Ash what she was being careful *not* to say. That Colonel Waterson had been on the front line a little too long before he'd got his commission and hadn't handled the transition to flying a desk well. It was the same unsettling battle Ash himself was now facing, but seeing how failure to get the balance right had led to some poor decisions on the former

Colonel's part, with tragic consequences, Ash knew it was imperative that he found a way to accept the monumental change his promotion had brought.

'Actually, I was hoping for your help in that,' he announced, firmly quashing any doubts that, if he wasn't yet playing with fire, he was most certainly toying with a full box of matches.

He didn't blame her for her suspicious frown but he had to clench his fist to stop himself from reaching out to smooth it away. Her skin looked silky-soft.

What would it be like to touch his lips to her, taste her?

'You want *my* help?'

'You were the one who noticed the men were beginning to close ranks, view others as outsiders.' He shrugged. 'You work with them on a daily basis and you clearly care deeply about your fellow soldiers. Why *wouldn't* I want your help?'

He could practically see her mind whirling, trying to decide whether he was serious. Whether she should acknowledge the sparks which, even now, arced between the two of them. They made his stomach pull taut, his chest swell; she made him feel like a horny kid again, but he was determined that if he ignored it long enough it would pass. It had to. He'd never allowed himself to be distracted from his Army career before and he wasn't about to start now.

His rank and reputation were all he had left.

Rosie might not be dead yet, but realistically he'd lost the only mother he remembered a long time ago. Pain seared through him but he thrust it viciously away. Waiting for the phone call to confirm it felt like losing her all over again. It was just another version of hell.

He would control it. Just as he always controlled his emotions these days.

Dragging himself back to reality, he was just in time to see Fliss peering crossly at his right shoulder. He resisted the urge to twist away, knowing it was too late.

'What's that?' she demanded.

He gritted his teeth. 'It's nothing.'

'There's a dark stain discolouring the fabric and it looks suspiciously like blood,' she accused. 'Did you think that just because it's called *multi-terrain camouflage pattern* I wouldn't spot it?'

'It's probably Corporal Hollings's blood.'

The dark look she cast him actually made him ache. It was as though she actually…*cared.*

Something inside him cracked. The faintest hairline fracture, but it was there all the same.

'What, *after* you've grabbed a shower and

changed? Anyway, the line's too neat for that. It looks as though someone's tried to patch it up and it has seeped through the sides of a bandage,' she said pointedly.

'I advise you to lower your voice,' murmured Ash, equally pointedly.

Her head jerked up sharply. He couldn't blame her; she'd hardly been shouting but he had no idea who else might be around. She cast him a disappointed gaze.

'Are you going to pretend you're fine? Because I can tell you now that the macho soldier doesn't impress me.'

'So you think I'm trying to impress you? Do I need to remind you that I may not be your CO, but I am still *a* CO?'

She flushed but stood her ground. It was a trait he'd got to know very quickly. And one he liked. A lot.

'As you wish, *Colonel*. But do I need to remind you that, CO or not, when it comes to medical issues I have ultimate authority, even over you?'

She was so damned sexy when she was being combative. As though she couldn't bear to relinquish control any more than he could.

'That doesn't change the fact that I'm not discussing this here.'

'So it *is* macho pride?' She shot him another

disappointed gaze. 'I was beginning to think better of you. But, either way, you *will* show me that wound, *Colonel*.'

Unexpectedly, she marched up the corridor, unlocked a supply room door and held it open with a jerk of her hand to command him inside.

'Or do I have to physically manhandle you in here?' she muttered.

He'd like to see her try. He swallowed down a wicked grin. Scratch that, he *wouldn't* like to see her try. He was barely controlling the impulse to pull her closer and kiss that defiant glower right off her delectable mouth as it was. Having her touch him, in any capacity, would be like striking the damn match.

He hesitated, then consented to enter the room, his voice low but clear.

'It's not about *macho pride*, as you call it. As you pointed out so succinctly yesterday, my men have already lost one colonel and morale is low. I don't want it sinking even further because they caught wind of some rumour that their new CO had also been injured.'

A pretty flush spread up and over her neck as she realised the truth of his words. Ash wasn't sure what was cuter, the Major mad at him or the Major embarrassed by him. Still, she recovered quickly enough. Or at least that was what she wanted him to think.

'What's more, injured on your first sortie,' she pointed out shakily.

He couldn't keep the wry tone out of his voice. 'Indeed.'

Checking the corridor, she closed the door behind them and gestured to him to join her beside a clear countertop.

'Take your shirt off, and whatever layers you're wearing underneath, and let me see that wound properly.'

So clipped, so professional, but Ash thought he heard the faintest quiver beneath. For a moment he debated the wisdom of being in this claustrophobic room, half-naked and alone with a woman he couldn't seem to keep his hands off, at least in the privacy of his own head.

And what about the scars?

He'd never worried about his scars before. He was an infantry soldier; other men who'd seen them knew better than to ask, and women who'd seen them had swallowed whatever superficial story he'd thrown at them.

But the Major?

Ash had a feeling she would be able to see right through him.

He locked his jaw irritably. Since when did it matter to him what she—what anyone— thought? Hooking his fingers under the layers, he pulled them over his head in one smooth movement before folding his arms, seemingly casually, over his chest.

With something approaching satisfaction, he heard the air *whoosh* out of her lungs, saw her pupils dilating as she backed up further. She was fighting it, this attraction. And yet, even as she did so, her eyes didn't stop raking over him, with the results as real as if she'd actually raked her fingernails across his skin instead. His body burned up with desire.

They just had to get through this before he gave in to his baser instincts and, for the first time in his career on an active tour of duty, mixed his Army life with his personal one.

Every time he thought he was back in control, she slipped beneath the surface and unravelled all his iron-clad control like a kitten would toy with a ball of yarn. Suddenly, he didn't want to fight it any more. He wanted to know how it would feel to give in—just this once—and steal one perfect kiss from those plump, quivering lips.

One kiss.

No, he'd survived ambushes, engaged in fifty-hour firefights and fought with the enemy in hand-to-hand combat. He'd pick any one of those over letting this woman get close enough to sneak behind his armour.

Just one kiss.

It was a constant battle between his baser instincts and his brain. *Only an animal couldn't control their baser instincts,* he warned himself contemptuously. Besides, this woman could hurt him more than any enemy could.

But just one kiss.

The man was magnificent.

Her heart couldn't work out whether to race or to miss beats, her eyes seemed riveted on the well-honed physique to which even her imagination hadn't done justice and her nostrils filled with a fresh, citrusy shower gel scent mingled with the undertones of leather. Ever since she'd mentioned the shower, standing back in that corridor, she hadn't been able to stop mentally placing him under the hot flow of water as it cascaded over those broad shoulders and down that all too sculpted physique. His proximity was so damned consuming.

'Can you see it from there, or are you going to come a little closer?' Deep and sensual, his voice reverberated through her, body-slamming her and sending heat pooling between her legs.

'I need supplies first,' she hedged.

Another eyebrow quirk. 'Without inspecting the wound?'

She felt decidedly rattled. Whatever had happened to 'stick of rock' Fliss, with Army Rules and Regulations stamped right through her? She scrambled for an excuse not to step closer until she was sure she wouldn't do something as improper as running her hands over him.

But what would it be like to feel those beautiful muscles bunching beneath her palms? Those calloused fingers grazing her soft skin?

'I can tell from here it's going to need suturing,' she lied, coughing to clear her throat.

In all her years within the military she had never—not once—fantasised about a fellow soldier. Fliss stopped abruptly.

Come to think of it, she had never in her life fantasised about anyone.

She hadn't been able to see what purpose a fantasy served. No one before had ever set her pulse racing or filled her with such a raw need that her whole body actually trembled at the thought of their touch.

And then the Colonel had come along and she'd stood in that tent and felt as though she'd been hit by an armoured tank. Being in the field with him and seeing him in action, working with him in such harmony as though they'd known each other for years, had only intensified the attraction.

She'd seen a fair few heroes in her role as an army trauma doctor, but the Colonel was the stuff of action films. And he had something more, something harder, some inner drive. She'd been given a taste of what he was capable of, how loyal he was, and the physical attraction had expanded into something more.

It frightened her even as it excited her.

He's just a man.

She tried to push the tumultuous emotions from her brain but, even now, he dominated the space, his backside resting on the countertop, his long, powerful legs stretched out in front of him, one ankle crossed casually over the other. Her heart hammered so fast she was surprised he couldn't hear it. She wanted to look away but she couldn't tear her eyes from his body. The tiny room practically pulsed with his dark, powerful energy, sliding under her skin and into her veins to flutter wildly at her neck. His eyes slid to her pulse as if he could read her thoughts, swiftly followed up with his lips thinning as if in distaste.

It was a rejection she recognised all too well.

Hurt cut through her. Enough to kick-start her sense of self-preservation. What was she thinking, imagining a guy like him could really be interested in someone like her?

Focus, Fliss.

'Right, let me inspect the wound,' she bit out, shaking back hair which wasn't there and advancing as confidently as she could, hands out-stretched.

He braced himself. Only a fraction of a second but she didn't miss it. Heat suffused her cheeks. He could read her silly schoolgirl crush and was embarrassed on her behalf. It was all she could do not to turn and flee.

Hauling her eyes to his shoulder, she saw where he'd tried to bandage the seeping wound, not wanting anyone to know about the injury. But, as neat a job as he'd managed, the damage beneath was clearly too deep. Carefully, she reached out and peeled away the dressing. At least her hands were steady, which was more than could be said for the rest of her.

'Jeez, what did you do?' she cried out, her eyes darting to his in horror.

'What does it look like? I tried to suture it.'

'Yourself? Without anaesthetic?'

He shrugged, ignoring the second question.

'I'm usually right-handed.'

'Yeah, because *that's* why it's bleeding.'

She stared into those shale-hued eyes and felt herself teetering *oh-so-close* to the edge. With a supreme effort she pulled herself back.

'I've had worse.'

She didn't doubt it.

'How did you get it?'

'Sliced it on some rusty metal when we were breaking down the door to that compound.'

She clucked her tongue, relieved at the banality of the exchange. At least it was keeping her mind distracted whilst they were so dangerously close to each other. She prattled on quickly to stop her voice, and hands, from shaking.

'So you're going to need stitches *and* a tetanus, but you weren't intending to come to me. What are you, some kind of idiot?'

'Careful, Major.' His low voice rumbled through her. 'I've let a lot slide because you're kind of sexy when you're bossy. But don't push it.'

He was right; it was no way to speak to a superior. Certainly no way Fliss would ever have previously dreamt of speaking to one. But nothing about him had her acting like normal and, despite her best efforts, he disconcerted her, leaving her jangling nerves needing an outlet.

Wait... He thought she was sexy?

Belatedly, her eyes snapped to his, her tongue flicking out to moisten her parched lips. His gaze pulled down to the movement.

'And that doesn't help.'

'What doesn't?'

Was that breathy sound really her voice?

They had inched closer. She hadn't noticed it,

but they had. Now the soft caresses of his shallow breaths tickled her cheek.

'Tell me how it is that you don't have a boyfriend or partner somewhere, worrying about you?'

Pain sliced through her more than she'd have wished. But, like every time before, it was about the sense of rejection rather than losing Robert himself.

What was so very wrong with her that the people who were supposed to care about her didn't think she was special enough for them to stay?

She took a step back from Ash, as though putting physical distance between them might ease the feelings of inadequacy. What if she told him and it caused him to think less of her as a woman?

'Who says I don't have someone?' She'd meant it to sound nonchalant but it just came out brittle, cold.

'If you did have someone, you wouldn't be here now,' Ash pointed out, unperturbed. 'You certainly wouldn't have allowed yourself to respond to me the way you do. However strong the attraction, you'd have shut it down back in your CO's office the other day.'

He was right; she would have.

'Fine,' she snapped. 'There's no one.'

'But there was?' he pushed, perceptively.

'It's none of your business.'

'Fair enough.'

'What about Simon?'

'Simon?' Fliss stopped her inspection and shot him an incredulous look.

'Your CO.'

'Yes, I know who he is.' She shook her head. 'There's nothing…like that going on.'

'He wouldn't mind if there was.'

'You're crazy,' Fliss snorted, wondering where that had come from. 'Besides, I don't do that.'

Before she could think anything else, however, Ash had slipped one arm around her waist, the other hand closing around her wrist, his legs parting as he pulled her in between them. She was far enough away that there was a clear gap between his body and hers, but so close she could almost feel him.

'Good to know,' he muttered.

She should push away. But she didn't. She couldn't resist him. Her body literally ached with the need to press against him. But, if she did, she was afraid she might forget all her principles entirely.

'I… I just said. I don't do this,' she choked out.

'Do what? *This?*'

His thumb pads stroked the inside of her wrists, causing her pulse to lurch yet again, and Fliss wondered if he could feel it. The silence hung between them, his heartbeat drumming steadily, strongly, beneath her palm as invisible threads seemed to wrap around them.

She was frozen. She knew she should pull away but she couldn't.

Someone was going to get hurt and she knew exactly who. But, even as she struggled to pull away, eyes the hue of mountain shale bound her tight, as entrancing and as perilous as a fathomless mine shaft. If she got too close to the edge she would tumble, and there would be no climbing out.

And still she didn't move away.

Slowly her hand lifted involuntarily to rest on his chest.

Another inch closer and his breath rippled over her lips, sending electricity *zinging* around her body. He was going to kiss her and she wasn't going to do anything to stop him.

So very close.

Fliss fought to harness her galloping heart as one hand still held her wrist as the other brushed up her body to cup her ribcage, his thumb grazing the underside of her breast whilst only barely touching.

And then, leaning forward, he brushed her lips with his own.

A small squeak escaped her lips.

'Oh.'

She was pretty sure she'd never squeaked in her life.

The heady mix of citrus and leather intensified and Fliss couldn't stop herself from wondering what his skin might taste like, how it would feel to graze her body against his. Her breasts felt strangely heavy, aching at the idea. But that was nothing compared to the flames licking around other parts of her body. It was like nothing she recognised.

Sex before had always been pleasant but perfunctory. She had a feeling *pleasant* was the last adjective a woman would use when describing sex with the Colonel. Her body shivered suddenly at all the adjectives she *could* imagine.

'What are you doing?' she murmured.

'I've no idea,' he admitted, running his thumb over her bottom lip, and then chasing it with his tongue. 'I just know I keep trying to resist you but then I find myself crossing the line I've always drawn in my head.'

Molten heat bubbled up inside her. The idea of pushing a man as virile as this over any line was exhilarating. Could he really want her that badly? It offered an odd sense of power. Almost a validation as a woman. And right now that was something she was sorely lacking.

Frightened of talking herself out of it, Fliss abruptly closed the gap between them. His evident arousal let her know in no uncertain terms just how badly he wanted her. Fire whipped through her and she shifted against him, hearing the moan in the back of his throat as he lifted his hand to cradle the back of her neck, his other hand cupping her backside as he pressed her even more tightly against him.

Instinctively, she parted her legs slightly, rocking against him, revelling in his low groans and her own soft sighs. And then he slipped his lips from hers, kissing along her jawline to the dip beneath her ear as his hand dropped from her neck to her breast, cupping it in one solid palm as he raked a thumb over the nipple. Even through her uniform it sent another hot stab rushing to her core. But she wanted so much more.

'Colonel...'

'Given the circumstances,' he murmured, his words trailing over her lips, 'I think calling me Ash might be more appropriate.'

'Ash...' She rolled the name around her tongue, liking the way it felt on her lips.

Finally slipping her wrist out of his grasp, she flattened her palm on his shoulder, careful to avoid the wound she hadn't even got around to dealing with yet, and let her palm graze down over his body.

It was even more incredible beneath her touch. Muscles bunched and tensed as she teased him, and he got his delicious revenge by dropping white-hot kisses into the hollow of her neck. She traced lower and lower, until she felt the edges of scars.

They went on for ever.

Surprised, she pushed back from him, her legs staying where they were but enough to dip her head to see. His whole body had tensed, his grip that little bit tighter on her body.

'What happened?'

'Grenade,' he answered simply.

So that was how he wanted to play it?

'Must have been some grenade.'

'I'm still alive,' he bit out. 'Body armour took the brunt of it.'

She could tell that wasn't exactly true and, in any case, body armour caused problems of a different kind. But Fliss said nothing; instead she traced the scars, the damaged tissue, the skin grafts. Up to his pectoral muscles, across his abs towards the line of hairs to his belly button, down over his lower abs until it dipped down beneath his waistband, where she couldn't trace it any further. Then her hands skimmed over to the insides of his forearms.

Small, circular scars, too regular in shape. She'd seen it before, but on a guy like *this*?

She snapped her head up to make direct eye contact.

'And these?'

Ash thrust her away from him so fast she almost stumbled backwards. He made no move to catch her, only folded his arms across his chest, those biceps bulging all the more, and glowered at her.

'Just get the suture kit and do your damned job, *Major*, if you can keep your hands to yourself for that long. Then we can both get the hell out of here.'

CHAPTER FOUR

'WHAT HAVE WE GOT?' Fliss jumped off the heli to speak to the medic on the ground as her team hauled the casualty on board.

'Fusilier Bowman, nineteen, was playing football with the local lads when two of them had a collision and Bowman fell on his shoulder and broke his clavicle.'

Already she could see her team checking the airway, breathing, and circulation, one of her crew moving behind the casualty to examine the clavicle itself, including any signs of deformity.

'Oscillate and percuss the lung fields to exclude pneumothorax and carry out a neurovascular examination, particularly for upper limb pulses, decreased perfusion and muscle power,' she called out. 'Okay, let's see the other lad involved.'

A brief check confirmed the other player had got off lightly. More than likely the break had occurred on impact with the ground rather than with the other player. Still, Fliss wanted to rule out the possibility of a head injury.

Satisfied, she was on her way back to the heli when a voice halted her.

'Ma'am?'

Fliss stopped, turning to the trio of soldiers eagerly approaching.

'We heard Colonel Stirling is in Razorwire now; he was on a MERT shout yesterday?' one of them asked.

Fliss nodded, wishing her whole body didn't react at the mere mention of his name.

'Are you likely to see him, ma'am?'

She plastered a pleasant smile on her lips. 'Doubtful, gents. Sorry.'

'Oh.'

The lads looked disappointed, and before she knew it she was being drawn in.

'Why?'

'It's just that… Would you just tell him…?'

'That it's a bit quiet here without him,' the second lad interjected.

Fliss pressed her lips together. It wasn't what the lads were saying so much as what they *weren't* saying. This was the closest these guys got to saying they missed someone. It said a lot about the Colonel. Her expression softened.

'He was your company commander?'

'No, ma'am.' The second lad shook his head. 'He was only a captain when we knew him, our recce platoon commander. Before he got himself blown up.'

Her heart bounded around her ribcage.

'The grenade? You were there?'

They looked like kids.

'Yeah, of course. Six years ago. The boss saved our lives,' the first lad announced proudly. 'Mick, Jonesy and me, ma'am. And some others who are going to be mad they aren't here now.'

'I see,' she acknowledged. 'I knew the Colonel had been involved in a grenade incident but I'm afraid I don't know the details.'

'Let me guess, the boss doesn't like to talk about it, ma'am? Claims it was no big deal and he was just doing his job? That sounds about right.'

'You don't agree, gentlemen?'

'No, ma'am, we don't,' the second lad declared. 'A bunch of us wouldn't be here without him.'

Their pride and admiration was infectious and Fliss couldn't help herself. She could pretend it was professional interest. She knew better.

A few days ago she wouldn't have even considered discussing Ash's injury but, after what had happened in the supply room, she couldn't shake the part of her which was desperate to know more.

'I understand the injury is extensive; the blast got under the body armour.'

'Yeah. We'd been ambushed, ma'am, pinned down in a small courtyard. He had about six seconds between the grenade rolling in and it going off to make a decision. If he'd told us to make a run for it we'd have all got caught by the blast or the shrapnel. But the boss being the boss, he grabbed a small daysack, threw it on the grenade and threw himself on top of that.'

'He was in pretty bad shape, ma'am,' another confirmed. 'Aside from the blast injuries themselves, he had some twenty fractures or breaks from the body armour. We didn't think he was going to make it.'

'He got transferred out and I think he was recovering for about a year, ma'am, before they placed him with a new unit and made him fly a desk for three years. I think he hated every second of it.'

Fliss absorbed all the information. It certainly explained why he was finding it so hard to work in the new role as colonel, as well as why he had such an impressive reputation. But, before she could answer, one of the QRF ran over to her.

'Reports coming in of another shout,' he yelled, as Fliss had already started running alongside him back to the heli.

'A series of explosions involving gas canisters used by the local school for cooking. Multiple casualties, they're sending both MERTs out. Kids were caught in the first blast and locals and soldiers there as rescuers in the second blast.'

'Fine,' she yelled as she leaped back on board. 'We'll take this casualty back to camp and head straight back out.'

All she could do was hope against hope that it wasn't as bad as it sounded.

Ash spotted her the moment he reached the rooftop, her hunched up shape silhouetted against the horizon as she sat in solitude watching the last of the sunset over the desert.

'They said you'd be up here.'

If she heard his voice, she didn't react.

He inched along the concrete terrace, ducking low until he reached her. Her shoulders stiffened awkwardly as she finally turned, discreetly brushing at her cheeks as though they were damp and wiped a finger under each eye. Something twisted inside him to see her in distress.

'Mind if I sit down?'

There was a moment of hesitation before she inclined her head, but they both knew he'd have sat anyway.

'Want to talk about it?'

Another hesitation and this time she shook her head.

'Okay,' he acknowledged, folding his arms and allowing them both to lapse back into silence.

But at least now she wasn't alone.

He'd heard about the incident and could well imagine the grim scenario. He knew that was why she was up here alone, to vent some emotion in private without bringing down the morale of the rest of the camp. The other members of her team could console each other but he knew Fliss would feel that, as their major and leader, she had to stray strong. She could be there for them, but not the other way around.

An ingrained sense of responsibility and duty. Just like her uncle, the General. Just like *him*. He should respect that. He should just tell her the little sliver of good news he had and then he should leave.

He didn't get involved, he reminded himself brutally.

'Anyway—' Ash broke the silence '—I came up here to tell you about Corporal Hollings—the soldier from the RTA yesterday?'

'I remember who Corporal Hollings is.' She nodded quietly. 'Andy Hollings.'

Ash wasn't surprised. He had a feeling she remembered every single soldier she rescued.

All her casualties mattered to her. Not that he hadn't met plenty of trauma doctors who cared before now, but there was something...*more* about Major Felicity Delaunay.

'I figured it must be pretty unpleasant sometimes, being on the MERT. You see those who don't make it, but you never get to find out what happens to those soldiers you keep alive long enough to get to the hospital.'

'Yeah, sometimes,' she agreed jerkily. 'The rush of saving a life is the greatest feeling and I love my job, I wouldn't change it for the world. But sometimes...'

'Yeah, so I thought you'd like to know that Hollings' operation went well yesterday. He'll be stable enough to be leaving on a plane back to the UK hospital within the next twelve hours. He's still alive, thanks to you.'

'And you. If you hadn't got us into that shelter...'

'We made a good team.'

He didn't realise how intimate that would sound until the words were out. Yet with anyone else it wouldn't have held any deeper significance. By the loaded silence, Fliss thought the same.

'Thanks,' she managed at last. 'I mean, for coming to tell me.'

'No problem.'

Another silence pressed in on them. He ought to leave. He straightened his legs, ready to get up.

'Wait.'

He paused. Stopped.

'How did you know about Andy Hollings?'

Ash didn't know how best to answer her.

'It's not as though you're around the hospital much.'

'I just happened to be there,' he offered.

Her shrewd look seemed to pierce through him, boring into his armour, creating cracks where none should be.

'Do you mean you went in there specifically to check on the lad's progress? You couldn't just leave it, could you? You hoped he had pulled through the operation.'

'It isn't a big deal.'

She clicked her tongue. 'They *really* were right about you.'

'Don't read so much into it,' he warned uneasily. 'Who was right?'

'No one, forget it.'

Ash clenched his jaw. The problem was that her looks, her words, her touch, all chipped away at the guise he had painstakingly built up over the years. She was getting behind it and reaching for the man in there and he was finding it harder and harder to resist.

But he had to resist. He was having enough trouble resisting the physical attraction as it was, without her throwing in the dangerous complication of emotions.

He should leave. He'd said what he'd come up to say. Ash tried to make a move but a heaviness had set in, bone-deep, and he stayed exactly where he was.

'I've never seen the sunset from this height before,' he commented, his tone deliberately casual. 'It's impressive.'

'It's beautiful,' she muttered. 'I've taken several photos over the last few months. And this is one of several safe rooftops around camp—at least for now. Back when I was still in training, I used to have to go to a FIBUA training area back home, near where I lived. We had exercises where the soldiers would be practising their Fighting in Built-Up Areas skills, and doing casualty evacuation scenarios, and I would play out treating the casualty. I…didn't have the best childhood so I've always found it hard to talk to people. But there was a rooftop similar to this— different view, of course—which was deserted after hours so it always seemed such a peaceful place to go in order to think, to process.'

He couldn't help it. Instantly, Ash wondered what had happened in her childhood. He could bet it hadn't been anything like his. A kid like her, with a general for an uncle and Army blood running through her veins, always destined to be a commissioned officer, wouldn't know what a bad childhood was. Not the way he did. Not the way a huge number of the infantry soldiers, still kids themselves, did. He waited for the habitual bristle of resentment which always seemed to get to him when people who'd had it relatively easy thought they'd had it bad.

But for once it didn't come. Instead, he found himself trying to empathise with her. Trying to see that it was all relative and, from her point of view, it *might* have felt like a difficult time growing up.

'You come up here to process events like today,' he repeated carefully. 'I understand that.'

She hunched her shoulders, neither confirmation nor rebuttal.

'It's more than that. One day at the FIBUA an over-eager soldier fell out of a second-storey window during a routine house clearance. I ended up treating a casualty for real and performed my first emergency tracheotomy. I saved my first life and I didn't freeze, I didn't panic. The adrenalin was pumping, yes, but other than that it just came naturally. It was the moment I realised I could really do it, I could be an army trauma doctor—I could be a *great* army trauma doctor. The rooftop was where I finally let go of the past and embraced a new, positive future.'

'So you come up here after bad days like today to try to recapture that sense of victory,' he realised.

'Yes,' she whispered. 'To remember what it feels like to get it right. Saving a life is a rush like no other; it's an unbeatable feeling. But losing one is devastating. And the nature of the MERT means that sometimes you lose more than you win.'

Yes, he could certainly understand that, just as he understood her need to come up here and have her moment of weakness out of sight of the others, her reluctance to shed a tear in front of her team. He understood her sense of propriety that, as their team leader and a major, she should stay strong for them.

It was a degree of staying in control he recognised all too well.

So why was he still up here instead of leaving her alone?

Because he felt as if he could help her, Ash realised. Some part of him *needed* to help her. It wasn't about this inexplicable chemistry between them, although that had probably been the catalyst. It was about the way they had *clicked*, working in the field together the previous day. In all his experience, he had never fallen into such harmonious synchronicity with someone in such a short time, almost pre-empting each other's needs as they'd worked towards the common goal of saving that corporal's life.

'Felicity, you know you did everything you could today. You…'

'We lost them all,' she choked out, interrupting him. '*All* of them. It wasn't enough.'

'And you aren't to blame,' he stated firmly.

She didn't answer immediately, simply stared angrily out over the sunset. When she did finally speak, her voice was little more than a whisper.

'It's bad enough when it's a warzone. When there are IEDs and enemies. I've been to enough of them; I've dealt with explosions, and fatalities, and soldiers requiring multiple amputations. And all I can do, every shout, is know that I've done my utmost to get them back as much in one piece as I can.'

'I know,' he murmured reassuringly.

Her voice was choked and he knew she was close to the edge. He had no idea why, but he found himself putting his arm around her shoulders and drawing her in. She stiffened at first, resisting him, and then allowed herself to be shifted, still fighting to hold back her sense of failure.

'But here we're not in a warzone. It was an

avoidable accident and it killed so many. And there was no one I could help. Not a single person. Not even one child.'

Before he could stop himself, or tell himself that this wasn't keeping control of his emotions around her, Ash twisted her around to cradle her. It was more than a colonel being there for another soldier, it was personal, and inappropriate, and dangerous.

He rubbed his hand up and down her back to soothe her. And for several long minutes she let him.

Finally, as the tears subsided and she fought to regain control, she shifted away from him as he reluctantly let her go. A dark shadow he didn't care to identify stole over his chest, pulling a tourniquet around his guts and clenching his fist.

He rubbed a hand over his face. For two people who valued their self-control, neither of them seemed to have been doing particularly well since they'd met.

What was it about this woman that was so different to anyone else?

For years he'd succeeded in keeping people at arm's length, maintaining a barrier between himself and the rest of the world. Only Rosie and Wilf had been the exception. He'd known that the only sure-fire way never to lose control of his emotions, the way his father had, was to ensure he didn't let people close enough to generate those emotions in the first instance.

Yet here he was, on the roof with a woman he'd met barely seventy-two hours earlier, wondering what it might be like to have someone like this in his life. To have a bond with her that was more than the one they'd forged out there in the field the previous day.

She turned to him, then returned her gaze to the front. He twisted again to study her elegant profile—the long neck whose sweet scent he could still recall if he closed his eyes.

'So are you here as Colonel Stirling, CO of the QRF team? Or Ash, the man who nearly kissed me in that supply room yesterday?' she managed hoarsely, still not turning to face him again.

'Whichever you'd prefer.' Ash kept his voice low and even, blocking out the fact that the same question was tumbling around his own head.

Why had he felt so compelled to seek her out?

Part of him wondered if it had anything to do with the news he'd received today about his foster mother. Something threatened to bubble up inside him, and Ash swiftly closed it down to concentrate on Fliss. Willing her to give him the answer he shouldn't want to hear.

The silence felt like an eternity.

'Tell me about the grenade scar,' she said quietly, by way of response.

He stuffed down the black storm which immediately began to batter the lid of the box he kept it in. Only this time it didn't seem to rage with quite the power it had in the past.

'I told you, it was nothing.'

'So you say, but I ran into some of your old platoon in the field, and they didn't seem to think it was nothing.'

Ash frowned. 'My old platoon?'

'Mick, Jonesy and another guy...they called him Donald but I don't think that was his name.'

The names rushed through his head, leaving a trail of memories in their wake.

'Donaldson,' Ash said quietly. 'His younger brother had died in an ambush a couple of months earlier.'

'I'm sorry; I didn't know.'

'How could you have?'

'They told me you saved their lives, throwing yourself on a grenade.'

He stared at the sun, now so low behind the horizon that it was becoming quite dark up on the roof.

'I happened to be closest.' Ash shrugged. 'Any one of them would have done the same.'

'They said you'd say that.'

'Because they know it's true.' Ash brushed it off easily.

Fliss flashed him a sudden, genuine smile, and it was as though the sun had sprung back up into the sky again. It dazzled him, flowed into him, and filled him with light which chased down to even the darkest corners.

'Maybe,' she said. 'What about the other scars?'

The flooding light inside him pulled up sharply and began to recede. They both knew which scars she meant. He'd never told anyone about them before—except for the army doctor, of course—and he didn't particularly want to now. He'd faced the enemy and been hopelessly outnumbered on countless occasions in his career. He'd been cornered in the most brutal firefights and he'd had to escape and evade in the most hostile of environments.

But he'd take any one of those situations over facing down this resilient woman any day.

Except that Fliss was asking him to trust her, and he had an inexplicable urge to keep being honest with her. He liked the way it made her look at him, the way she responded to him. She was challenging him to open up—the one thing he couldn't afford to do. It would make him vulnerable, and he never wanted to be that again.

He pulled his lips into a tight line, determined

to quell the storm inside him so that when he stood up to bid her farewell he wouldn't betray himself. He wouldn't reveal the quagmire of emotions raging within.

But before he could speak, Fliss did.

'Tell me about the cigarette burns, Ash.'

His world stopped.

And then started spinning. Wildly. Frighteningly. Out of control.

'If you already know what they are, then what's to tell?' he bit out.

But still he didn't stand up. He didn't leave.

She sucked in a breath. 'Who did that to you?'

He glowered into the night.

'Please Ash, talk to me.'

He shouldn't. But the compulsion to answer her, the *need* to answer her, was too strong.

'Foster mother.'

She didn't gasp; she didn't need to. Her shock and distaste radiated from her.

'How long were you in foster care?' she asked at last.

In the distance the flash of a headlight rounded a hillside, a local vehicle crawling along the dirt road. It provided him with a welcome distraction but no real relief.

'I was shuttled between care homes, foster homes and my old man from the age of about seven.'

He heard the steel edge in his voice, felt the way she flinched on his behalf, as though it had cut her personally. He didn't know what to think. To feel. So he did what he did best and he shut down the side of himself which held the awful memories and just focused on the basic facts themselves.

It was the only way to avoid losing control.

'What about the stab wound?'

'That one was a wallboard saw.'

'A what? Your foster mother again?'

'No. Foster father. Different family. Earlier time.'

'What happened?'

Ash shrugged before realising she probably couldn't see him. And still he kept his voice as neutral as possible.

'He was a gambler. And a heavy boozer. Probably lost at the former and so didn't have enough money for the latter. I was late in from my paper round—I used to do two but he didn't know about the second—and he was waiting for my weekly pay so he could go to the pub.'

'How many foster families?'

Ash could hear the horror in her voice. He steeled himself but still he was finding it harder and harder to stay detached. He could hear the incredulity in her voice and something twisted inside him. Why had he told her? The last thing he wanted was for her to look down on him. As people had looked down on him when he was a kid.

'Too many to remember, but they weren't all like that.'

'Still…'

He cut her off, not wanting to hear it since he couldn't change it.

'We can't all come from army blood and boarding schools.'

He actually felt her flinch beside him.

'It wasn't like that,' she bit out.

'But your parents never hurt you.'

It was a statement rather than a question, and he could almost hear the unspoken accusation in his tone.

Why was he getting angry with her?

It wasn't her fault his life didn't match hers. Ash shook his head. For over a decade he'd had a chip on his shoulder the size of a surface-to-air missile launcher, but he thought he'd managed to get rid of it over the years, as he'd progressed through the ranks and begun to accept himself for who he was. Somewhere along the line he'd realised his own worth.

Yet this one woman made him re-evaluate himself, and where his life was heading.

'I don't know who my father is and whilst my

mother never physically hurt me the way you were hurt, she wasn't…kind.'

The words were uttered so quietly, he almost missed them at first. But the bleakness cut into him.

'But your uncle, the General?' People rarely caught Ash out.

He didn't like the feeling. When your life depended on judging people and situations quickly and accurately, it was a skill you learned to hone early on.

'My uncle tracked us down when I was eight and told my mother it was no place for a kid.' The admission was grudging; she clearly felt her past was her own business. 'He gave her an ultimatum. Either she came home to my grandparents with me, or my uncle would take me away.'

'So you and your mother ended up living with your grandparents.'

'No. She told him to take me. The next time I saw her was when I was eleven and she needed money. Anyway, this isn't about me. This is about you. Or is this what you do? Turn a conversation around any time it gets too close for comfort?'

Ash opened his mouth then closed it again, fighting back the overwhelming need to know more about Fliss. To understand her better. She was nothing like the picture he'd built in his head, and he was suddenly desperate to uncover the real woman behind the Major.

But she was right. Normally, turning the conversation onto the other person was *exactly* how he dealt with this kind of scenario. Instead, he fought the impulse. This conversation had started with her asking about him. If he wasn't willing to open up to her then how could he expect her to trust him?

'What do you want to know?' he heard himself asking.

She hesitated for a moment. 'I asked how many foster families you lived with.'

Ash sucked in a silent breath. 'Quite a few. I was seven when I first went into care and stayed there for about nine years, on and off.'

'Why? What about your family?'

He thought he'd hardened himself to all these memories a long time ago. Now, he was beginning to realise he'd buried them only just below the surface and a couple of questions from Fliss threatened everything.

'Until I was six, home life was good. Great. My parents were good, kind. They worked hard, were proud of our home and every bit of family time we had was spent doing something together, from playing football in the park to teaching me how to build a homemade telescope.'

'My uncle did that once.' He could hear the soft smile in her tone.

'When I was six, my mum was diagnosed with advanced ovarian cancer and that year she died. My dad couldn't handle it. He didn't deal with her death; he didn't even talk about her after that day. He was too proud to ask for help. He lost his job, couldn't pay the bills, forgot to buy food or clothing, or even soap. He did, however, discover alcohol. By the time I was seven, we had lost our home and social services took me away. I got my first taste of foster care after that.'

'I thought there were many good foster families out there. I used to dream of being taken in…before my uncle finally rescued me.'

'Oh, don't get me wrong.' Ash hunched his shoulders. 'I had several placements which were okay. And there *are* lots of kind families. Some are even exceptional. But there simply aren't enough foster carers and the better they are, the more valuable they are in dealing with troubled kids. I wasn't considered in that category at first.'

'At first?'

'Every so often my dad would get his act together and I'd go back to him. But I don't know whether it was because I was too sharp a reminder of my mother or what, but at some point or other he'd slide back down and the cycle would start over. By the time I was thirteen I'd had a couple of bad homes and I'd fallen in with the wrong crowd in school—not that we were ever in school. At fourteen I was completely off the rails. That was when I got busted by the cops for boosting a car.'

Fliss was actually facing him now, her body turned to his, intent on what he had to say. Her compassion was palpable. Somewhere, deep inside his being, something in Ash twisted and broke away.

'That was when I got sent to my last foster family. They were in their sixties and they were...*different*.'

'Different?'

He could hear the suspicion in her voice. Almost as though she *cared*. His chest pulled tight.

'Rosie and Wilfred saved my life,' Ash clarified simply. 'Figuratively and literally. They pushed me, challenged me, refused to give up on me. Both of them, but especially Rosie. She made me take a long look at where my life was heading and whether I really wanted to be going in that direction. And then she helped me find a way to turn things around. I owe her—I owe them both—everything.'

Even in the darkness he could sense the questions which jostled on her lips. It felt unexpectedly good to have someone pushing him to talk.

'But that was over two decades ago. Ten years ago Rosie started suffering from Alzheimer's and ten months ago she was diagnosed with pancreatic cancer. A week ago they sent her home to…be with family.'

'Oh, Ash, I'm so sorry.'

'It is what it is.' He shrugged, grimly holding back the emotions which threatened to rush him. Especially at the empathy in her tone. 'I was never meant to be out here; I was to take up the post of CO once the battalion returned from Razorwire. But then Colonel Waterson's accident left them without a colonel and I came out for the men, for their last ten days.'

'They couldn't let you be home with her?' Fliss asked, aghast. 'Surely, if they'd known? The Army have contingencies for circumstances like these.'

'It makes no difference,' Ash cut in. 'I'm no use there anyway. Because of the Alzheimer's she doesn't know who I am. And I'm better out here. It's the right choice all round.'

'I really am sorry.'

Her concern, so obviously genuine, slammed into Ash, hard. He had never told anyone any of that, preferring to compartmentalise his emotions so that he could do the job he needed to do when he was on the front line. But here, in Razorwire, everything seemed to have a slightly softer focus to it, from the camp to the people. And especially Major Felicity Delaunay.

She seemed to have a habit of getting under his skin and chipping away at the armour he'd spent so many years hammering into place.

She threatened the separation of his two worlds, all endless legs and lithe body as she danced in and out of his thoughts on a daily basis, especially when he was stuck behind that desk trying to get to grips with his new job.

He had never, in fifteen years, lost control as he had that day in the supply room. She made his body thrum with desire simply by standing a couple of feet away. And if he didn't want to lose control again, then Ash knew there was only one thing he had to do.

Stay well away from Major Felicity Delaunay.

CHAPTER FIVE

FLISS SHIFTED ON the cot-bed—which was currently doubling up as a rickety sunbed—in the quiet nook she and Elle had discovered shortly after arriving at Razorwire. Tucked away between the accommodation shipping containers and the wall of a compound, it was one of the few wonderfully secluded areas on Camp. At least, one that wasn't on a rooftop.

Usually she revelled in the searing kiss of the sun on her skin, coursing through her body to heat her very bones. Today it just made her feel restless. It wasn't the sun's kiss she wanted on her. Despite the heat, goosebumps spread over her torso, her breathing catching at the memory.

Why couldn't she get Ash out of her head?

It didn't seem to matter how many times she reminded herself that Ash wasn't the uncomplicated, steadfast guy she needed, nothing seemed to settle her body's ache to feel his touch again.

More importantly, it didn't matter how many times she reminded herself that *she* wasn't what *Ash* wanted, that he had rejected her, it didn't diminish her attraction to him. And that knowledge caused a perpetual maelstrom to rage in her mind. Because, of all people, she knew how utterly painful it was to be rejected over and over again. Even now she kept hoping each sporadic visit from her mother would be different. And each time it wasn't she suffered a fresh rejection, and the black void in Fliss's heart grew that little bit deeper.

So why was she still even entertaining thoughts about Ash after he'd pushed her away so categorically in the supply room barely a week ago?

She shifted on the sunbed, finding it impossible to get comfortable. She already knew the answer to her own question; she just didn't want to acknowledge it. Doing so would only raise twice as many issues again. But she couldn't shut her mind off.

The truth was that she didn't *feel* rejected. If anything, it had felt more about *his* baggage than hers. He'd been the one trying to protect himself when she'd asked about the burn scars. Hadn't he come up on that roof to seek her out? Hadn't he told her about the scars? Hadn't he opened up to her?

The fact that he hadn't tried anything on was a good thing. It meant he truly had trusted her without it being a ploy to get her into bed.

Right?

She couldn't even talk to Elle, who had headed back home for a two-week R&R, and without her friend Fliss felt lost. She tried to recreate the conversation in her head, but she wasn't sure she would even have told her best friend about the encounter with Ash.

It was like a little secret that only she knew, and she hugged it to herself as though sharing it would make it pop and disappear like an ethereal bubble in the air. It felt special and fragile, but if she wanted it to have the chance of any more substance then she was going to have to do something about it. In two days' time she would be gone and the decision would have been made for her.

She sat bolt upright on the sunbed, perturbed at the thought. It seemed like such a waste. Such a squandered opportunity. So what was the alternative? Breaking every rule she had by seeking Ash out to give in to a moment of temptation which would hold no promises, and no future? A fortnight ago she would have scorned the very idea, but now even one night together seemed almost worth it. If only she could find some way to ring-fence her heart.

She reached for the bottle of sunscreen, applying it as though it could do more than protect merely her skin.

If only it was that easy.

Lost in her thoughts, Fliss missed the soft footfalls of a jogger approaching until the figure stopped abruptly, casting a long shadow over her torso and legs. She squinted, lifting one ineffectual hand against the bright sun, even though its glare was too bright for her to see. But she didn't need her eyes to tell her who it was. Her body seemed to know, every delicately fine hair on her body prickling in awareness.

Flustered, she stood up so quickly that she almost toppled. But, unlike in the supply room, this time strong arms steadied her in an instant. She reached out instinctively to brace herself, her hands connecting with one very hot, solid, familiar bare chest.

'Ooomph!'

'Easy, you'll cause yourself injury,' Ash murmured as Fliss's entire body seemed to tingle beneath his unabashed, and unmistakably male, appraisal.

And all her courage seemed to float into the air above their heads like a bunch of bobbing balloons and disappear before she could snatch it back.

She snapped her arms across her chest, all too conscious of the revealing, fire-engine-red bikini Elle had loaned her when they'd first discovered the quiet sunbathing spot. The barely-there two-piece, though perfect for her friend's lean, athletic B-cup body shape, felt entirely too scant on her own more curvaceous D-cup figure. She tugged at the material but that only seemed to make the problem worse.

'What are you doing here, Colonel?' she blurted out. 'First the rooftop, now here? Are you following me?'

It was a daft accusation, a defence mechanism to try to hide her embarrassment, and she wanted to swallow it back the moment it left her lips. But, far from goading him, he actually looked amused.

'No one's around, Felicity; have you forgotten my first name?'

Despite herself, a delicious shiver rippled through her. She tugged again at the material.

'And you might want to stop doing that.'

His voice rasped across her belly, carnal lust heating between her legs and making her nipples harden until they were almost painful. When she looked at him, it was clear he hadn't missed her body's reaction to him and his shale-coloured eyes were almost black with desire.

'Why?' She swallowed.

'Because you're clearly fighting a losing battle and if you continue then those flimsy straps of yours are going to give way entirely. Those two pathetic triangles of cloth are no match for such…*generous* contents. It's a matter of physics.'

With anyone else, Fliss knew she would have prayed for the dusty ground to open up and swallow her. Her mother had told her that they were unattractively oversized, unsuitable for a dancer, and made her look fat. But the gravelly lust in Ash's tone, raw and unrestrained, suggested a different story. No man had ever spoken to her in quite that tone. It made her feel attractive, glamorous, even sexy.

Something ignited deep inside Fliss. It was like a sign. In two days' she'd be out of here. Tonight was her last chance to do something utterly out of character with the only man who had ever dislodged her professional mask.

If she didn't stop jiggling those incredible breasts around, he was seriously going to lose it.

Ash shifted as discreetly as he could—he was so aroused it was a kind of torture—and he had never been more grateful for his slightly baggy cargo running shorts as he stood, his hands still seared to her bare flesh. Surely no red-blooded male could watch that provocative show without having such a primal reaction? And what made it all the more arousing was the fact that

such a stunning woman could be so wholly un-
aware of just how incredibly sensual she was.

He would stake his life that the bikini didn't
belong to Fliss. From the colour to the cut,
it just didn't seem like something she would
choose for herself. But she looked absolutely
sensational in it. Then again, she looked equally
stunning in even the most unflattering army
uniform, complete with dusty body armour. All
of which would be considerably harder to divest
her of than those three scraps of siren temptation which wouldn't even stand up to the brief-
est run-in with his teeth.

A ferocious need pounded inside him. An
urge to touch her, taste her, every last hot, slick
inch of her. So much for his promise to himself
that he would avoid her for the couple of days
until the end of her tour. With a supreme effort,
Ash dropped his grip and stepped away from
her as casually as he could.

It was a mistake.

Instead of lowering the sexual tension, it only
seemed to increase it as he was treated to the
full head-to-toe effect of Fliss's body. She had
the softest, most feminine curves he thought
he'd ever seen. Not to mention a backside that
was so perfect he ached to cup it as he pulled
her against him.

What the heck was wrong with him?

She swallowed hard before speaking, her voice loaded with intent.

'Going somewhere?'

Ash could only cock an eyebrow in response. Had any other woman ever had quite this overpowering effect on him?

'Be very careful, Felicity,' he warned.

'Why do you say that?'

She took a step towards him but the slight quiver behind the seductive tone only confirmed his suspicion.

'Because I can't offer what you want.'

'I think you can.'

Another step. His body tightened further but he valiantly ignored it.

'I can't give you more than sex.'

'Who says I want more than that?'

'You did. When you told me you didn't do *this*, remember? But I don't go for meaningful relationships, I don't do intimacy. I *just* do sex.'

Fliss closed the gap between them, so close they could have touched if either of them had raised their arms.

'I know,' she murmured. 'Because sex is what you use as a defence against intimacy.'

Her gentle observation sliced right through him, hitting its mark. It certainly wasn't the first time he'd been accused of that. Just as he'd been accused of using his career and tours of duty to keep from putting down roots back home.

He could still recall every stage of his father's cycle of self-destruction when his mother had died. His father had lost all control, all reason, and he hadn't cared who he hurt in the process. Even a six-year-old boy who was trying to cope with the loss of his mother.

Ash couldn't remember how old he'd been when he'd sworn to himself that, whatever happened to him for the rest of his miserable life, he refused to become like his father. He would never let anyone close enough to be so torn apart by their loss. That way, he'd never be in so much pain that he'd hurt anyone, and he'd never, *ever* lose control.

'I don't want to have to think about someone else,' he lied, the proximity without contact only cranking up the sexual tension another intolerable notch. 'I'm an infantryman; my life is too dangerous to inflict on a girlfriend or a wife, and certainly not a family.'

'Rubbish,' Fliss retorted evenly, her hands finally raising to his chest, her fingers running gently over the contours of his body, tracing the ridges of the shameful circular scars as though she saw none of the ugliness behind them.

'You protect yourself because you had an appalling childhood and you got hurt. But I'm not asking you for more than you're willing to give, Ash. I'm accepting it will only ever be this moment between us.'

He needed to shut this down now. Keeping things as just sex would be one heck of a task. It would be so easy to fall for a woman as unique as Major Felicity Delaunay.

He moved to step away from her but instead Ash found himself placing his hands on her hips and drawing her close, her skin decadently smooth beneath his fingers. Then he hooked two fingers beneath her chin, tilting her head up to his as he lowered his mouth to finally claim hers the way he had back in that supply room what felt like an eternity ago.

Her lips parted for him with a soft sigh, her eyelids seeming to grow heavy as they fluttered closed and her body moulded to his, skin to skin but for her insubstantial bikini and his shorts. For now he resisted the urge to peel either away; he was barely holding onto his self-control with his fingertips as it was, and he could already feel Fliss's nipples through the material as her chest rose and fell with shallow breaths. Ash rubbed his thumb along her jawline before tugging the hair elastic from her ponytail and slipping his fingers into the silky curtain as it tumbled down, even richer and more luxuriant than he'd imagined it would be.

'So beautiful,' he marvelled, not merely referring to her hair.

The clipped sound she made was accompanied by her dragging his mouth back to hers and Ash indulged in the kiss without reservation, tasting every millimetre of her lips, her mouth, as her tongue danced with his in perfect synchronicity. She was clinging to him as if all the strength had gone from her legs, and it only made her feel all the more delicate in his arms.

Tantalisingly slowly, he allowed his hand to trace a line back to her chin, gliding slowly down her neck to the fluttering pulse, the smooth collarbone and the generous swell of breasts he ached to touch, to lick, to tease. With deliberate precision, he glided his hand down to cup one full breast and let his thumb sneak beneath the red triangle to graze over one straining peak.

Fliss trembled beneath his touch as she breathed his name with such bliss that he couldn't help himself. He lowered his head and took one peak in his mouth, his hand caressing the other. As she rocked her lower body against his there was no mistaking the heat emanating through the thin layers of material from her very core.

'Ash...please.'

White-hot need tore through Ash, infinitely

hotter than the sun beating down on their bodies. It would be so easy to tear off what remained of their clothes, wrap those endless legs of hers around his hips and thrust inside her. But if this was the one chance they were going to get then he owed it to both of them to make sure they didn't rush it.

He didn't hear his pager when it first went off, the sound slowly permeating through the hunger of their exploration. For a split second he was tempted to ignore it.

'You know I have to get that, don't you?' he managed hoarsely.

Reluctantly, Fliss released her grip and he eased her back, struggling to retrieve the pager, given her position and his arousal.

He shot her a rueful glance then checked his pager.

His blood ran cold, nausea surging and churning. When he finally spoke he didn't even recognise his own voice.

'I have to go.'

The message he'd been dreading had finally arrived.

CHAPTER SIX

FLISS SANK INTO the metal chair in frustration.

Delays weren't uncommon—especially during Relief in Place—with the sheer volume of air traffic, thanks to the change of troops at the beginning and the end of tours of duty, but she still didn't relish the prospect of being stuck at the Air Force base for the next thirty-six hours, waiting for a new part that had to be flown in for the aircraft.

At last they were finally out of the overheating tin can on the runway. Seven hours stuck out there in the blistering sun, after what was supposed to have been a brief, routine refuelling stop-over, had been quite enough.

But it wasn't just about where they were. Or the delay. It was the fact that Ash Stirling was still in her head. A dark bleakness stabbed at her. He hadn't sought her out the previous day. He hadn't summoned her. He hadn't even got a message to her. Something, anything, it wouldn't have mattered.

Logically, Fliss knew the way tasks were at

Camp Razorwire; they had a habit of swallowing up days before you even noticed it. But she couldn't shake the rejection and it attacked her more violently than it had in many, many years. It was over. Done. She needed to relegate to the past an imperfect experiment. But if she closed her eyes she could still feel the sheen of moisture on that impossibly hard body, take in the citrus and leather scent, hear the sensual huskiness of his voice.

Dragging herself back to reality as she exhaled a deep breath, Fliss pulled her bergen in between her legs and began to untie it to grab a couple of items packed closest to the top.

Regrets were useless; the situation had been taken out of their hands. She needed to straighten her head out. Starting with accommodation. Cotbeds had been set up in the neighbouring hangar and if she was quick enough she might even bag one of the choicest locations in the quietest corner.

'Ah, Colonel Stirling, your driver is ready to take you.' A voice from behind snagged her attention. 'You have a seat on the first direct commercial flight out of the main airport in the morning. Unfortunately, the airport hotel was already fully booked but I took the liberty of booking you into a hotel in the nearby tourist resort.'

'That sounds fine, Sergeant.'

If merely hearing his name had set the hairs bristling on the back of her arms, pausing in the action of retrieving her wash-bag, the sound of that rich, steady tone was enough to make her heart falter before galloping off.

What was he doing on a flight out of here too?

His infantry battalion wasn't due to leave for another week, which could only mean something bad. Without stopping to second-guess herself, Fliss stuffed the items haphazardly into the top of her rucksack, snatching at the closing ties and dragging it onto her shoulder as she sped across the floor.

'Colonel?'

There were too many soldiers around to risk using his first name but she trusted that he would see beyond the clipped tone. However, he didn't stop, striding confidently away from her and towards the main doors so that Fliss was forced to call again, barely concealing the note of panic in her tone.

To her relief he stopped, turning slowly, aviator-style glasses in his hand and an expression she didn't recognise cloaking his handsome face. She stopped abruptly, thrown. He looked like hell.

'Major?'

He was the very definition of poker-faced. She swallowed nervously. How was she supposed to do this with people all around them?

'I'm in a hurry,' he bit out. 'Walk with me.'

Without waiting for an answer, he turned and walked out of the doors, the wall of heat from outside hitting her despite the air-conditioning within the hangar. She stared after him, then her legs acted for the rest of her body, carrying her right along behind him. He'd walked to the end of the path to the road where the car was waiting for him. They'd moved out of the line of sight from the glass doors and no one was around.

'Is everything okay, Ash?'

Something flickered over his face, perhaps pleasure at seeing her, but then it changed to something she couldn't identify, and it was gone as quickly as it had arrived.

'I'm sorry I didn't get a chance to speak to you.' His clipped tone gave nothing away.

She waved it away as though it hadn't mattered.

'But are *you* okay?'

'Of course.' He hesitated a fraction too long. 'But I have some…loose ends to tie up in the UK. My promotion was never meant to take place until the battalion had returned from Razorwire; it just got accelerated after Colonel Waterson's accident.'

'You're booked on a commercial flight?'

'It's time sensitive.' He shrugged.

If she was overstepping, he didn't show it. In fact he showed no emotion at all. Unease rippled through her.

'Should I…would you like me to come with you?'

It had taken Fliss a lot to make the offer. The look he cast her was flat, expressionless. Her stomach pitched.

'Why would you do that?'

'Just to talk? Or…to finish the other day, if you like?'

Flat eyes stared at her. Then, all of a sudden, Ash's gaze turned hard and demandingly hot. It raked over her, as though virtually stripping her right down on the concrete. She could barely breathe, let alone move.

'You want to do that?' he demanded harshly.

'I want to,' she confirmed.

'All right, Major.' She hoped his use of her rank was because someone was approaching—his driver, perhaps. 'You can share my ride. Inform the duty sergeant and ask him to book you a flight and a hotel room.'

Had he misunderstood?

'Wait—' she lowered her voice '—I meant…'

Without warning, he pivoted, advancing on her so quickly they were almost toe to toe and she had to tip her head right back to look up at him. Every nerve-ending sizzled.

'I know exactly what you meant, Felicity,' he muttered under his breath. 'But if you want to keep the illusion of propriety, you'll want the duty sergeant to book you your own room with your own bed. Understood?'

'Understood,' she murmured in response.

He was so close she could feel his breath on her skin and the effect on her body was an immediate pooling of need between her legs. No man had *ever* affected her the way Ash did.

'Good. Then I suggest when I step away you look as though I have just given you a bit of a rollicking.'

'Right.'

Allowing him to step away, Fliss ducked her head and looked respectably contrite.

'Understood, Colonel, I'll deal with it right away.'

She turned to return to the duty sergeant at the desk.

'Leave your bergen here, Major.' He softened his voice just a fraction but it was enough to quell some of the fluttering in her chest. 'I'll get the Corporal to load it into the car while you make the arrangements. We don't have all day.'

* * *

'Major?'

Ash peered over his shoulder, not expecting to see Fliss's soundly sleeping form. He paused, catching his breath. She looked even more breathtaking in slumber than she did when she was awake, as though she didn't have a single care. Thick, dark lashes rested gently on her smooth cheek. Her breathing was slow and steady, for once not waiting to jerk awake at any unexpected disturbance.

Anger punched at his gut.

He shouldn't have agreed to this. He'd been in shock for the last two days, working on autopilot and remembering none of it. He'd only consented to her coming because the moment she'd stepped up to him in the hangar, the bright energy spilling from her had seemed like the very thing he needed to help him keep the darkness at bay. Without her, he knew it would engulf him and he didn't know if he'd ever make it back ashore.

Dragging her with him now was selfish and cruel. He was using her.

But if he made damn sure it was the best night of her life, then did it matter?

'Major—' he increased his voice whilst keeping it deliberately cool. 'Time to wake up; we're here.'

She finally stirred and offered a decidedly fe-
line stretch, and as the seat belt running down
the valley between her breasts grew taut, so did
Ash's body.

It was ridiculous, the effect she had on him.

But it was also exactly what he needed.

The last time he'd experienced such unrestrained lust he'd been sixteen and still dis-
covering the thrill of sex. Unsophisticated but
exhilarating. He'd soon unlocked the skill and
perfected the sophistication. But Fliss brought
back that youthful excitement—the innocence.

She peered out of the window then gazed
back at him through sleepy, lowered lashes,
which did little to calm his racing pulse.

'Already?' She looked shocked.

Second thoughts, perhaps?

Ash waited until the Corporal had climbed
out of the four-by-four and was headed around
to the back to collect their bergens before speaking urgently.

'If you've changed your mind, you can always go back.'

She could also stay in the room that the desk
sergeant had booked for her, but he didn't want
her to feel under any kind of misplaced obligation.

'I haven't changed my mind.' The gaze she
shot him was both loaded with promise and a

little nervous. 'I just expected the drive to feel a little awkward.'

So had he.

As the Corporal opened the back door, they both climbed out of the vehicle.

'Do I remember passing though somewhere and seeing a lot of floats, or did I dream that up?' she asked the young lad politely.

'It's Summer Festival time, ma'am,' the Corporal offered. 'Towns up and down the island celebrate in different ways. There's a parade with floats and live music and dancing not far from here tonight.'

'Really? It all looked beautiful.' She nodded. 'I've never been to a festival.'

'Never, Major?' Ash asked curiously, the suddenly pained expression in her eyes twisting at his gut, helping him to compartmentalise his own worries.

Already he was feeling more at peace than he'd felt in the last forty-eight hours.

'No.' She shrugged lightly, swiftly covering the moment.

He might tell himself it was none of his business but his mind kept asking questions.

Wordlessly, Ash reached for the rucksacks, passing Fliss hers as he hoisted his own onto his shoulder before thanking the young NCO and wishing him a safe return, then striding ahead into the cool hotel lobby to begin check-in. He couldn't even stop to see if Fliss was accompanying him. In uniform, and with the Corporal around, there was no place for chivalry.

Moments later he heard her greet the other receptionist at the far end of the four-metre-long desk and begin to confirm the booking the desk sergeant had made back at the airport base.

'I'm sorry you weren't able to get onto the six a.m. flight tomorrow morning with your colleague,' Ash heard the clerk saying.

'It's fine; don't worry.' Fliss's soothing smile carried in her tone. 'I was more than happy to get the early evening flight.'

'Still, the hotel would like to offer you a complimentary massage treatment in our spa, as well as use of our facilities even after the midday check-out.'

'Gosh, that's really kind of you,' she enthused in typical Fliss fashion. 'Thank you; I'd appreciate that.'

Images of Fliss's luscious body instantly flooded Ash's brain and he burned all over again, suppressing a grin. Yep, there was no denying that something about the woman transported him back to his teenage years.

His eyes slid across to hers for a fraction of an instant before she bowed her head with a flush. But not before he'd caught the sparkle of delight at his unrestrained interest.

Ash marvelled at the fact that neither Fliss herself, nor her fellow soldiers, appeared to be able to see past their perception of a prim, uptight, rigid rule-following major. There was so much more to the woman, so much raw passion, which bubbled away barely beneath the surface. She was like one of those papier-mâché volcanos Wilfred had taught him to make in their little man shed at the bottom of the garden. But instead of adding white vinegar to the bicarb mix to make it erupt, all Fliss would need would be a little love and the emotion would spill out of her.

Where the hell had that come from?

It was just another reminder that he should stop this now.

Instead, as though an invisible thread bound them, Ash concluded his check-in and moved along the desk to stand by her, his arm deliberately touching hers as he rested it on the granite surface. Unremarkable to any onlooker, but as his skin seared at the contact and goosebumps sprung up over Fliss's arm Ash experienced a renewed sense of satisfaction.

'I understand it's the Summer Festival across the island at the moment; we saw some floats on the way here?' He deliberately faced the clerk rather than Fliss.

'That's right, Colonel,' the young man agreed. 'There's a parade tonight. I could book you a taxi if you like; it's only about a ten-minute drive away.'

'What do you think, Major; shall we give it a go?'

'I…well… I thought this was about…?' With a subtle side-step she broke the physical contact and took a breath. 'If that's what you want, then we'll go.'

Relieved to occupy his mind, Ash narrowed his gaze at Fliss. Whatever made Fliss uncertain about going tonight, it wasn't just about wanting to finish what he'd started with her the other day. She was avoiding something.

The question was, what?

He'd spotted a moment of sheer longing in her regard when she'd mentioned the floats. As if it was something she wanted to see but couldn't bring herself to do.

He turned back to the young desk clerk. 'A taxi sounds fine.'

'Very good, sir. And will you be dining in the hotel restaurant?'

Beside him Fliss stiffened; evidently she preferred the structure of a known location. Yet another reason to change things up and see if he could get past those prickly defences of hers.

'No,' Ash decided. 'Thank you but I think we'll wing it and enjoy the festival atmosphere. Major, I'll be over by the lifts when you've concluded here.'

Before she could object to the change in evening plans he hoisted up the rucksacks, ignoring her attempts at a protest and leaving her with only a smaller one for appearance' sake. Then, making his way to the seating area, he watched her ramrod-straight back as she controlled her frustration, instead maintaining her charming smile for the clerk whilst she concluded her check-in.

By the time she finished and marched over he was already holding a lift for her and she stepped inside and pivoted stiffly around, opening her mouth.

'Which floor, Major?' he enquired politely, effectively cutting her off.

'Oh.' She halted, flipping the keycard over to check her room number. 'Fifth. Please.'

She waited for the lift doors to close before turning on him.

'Why did you do that?'

'Do what?' he asked innocently.

'Decide we should go to the parade?'

'Don't *you* want to?' He kept his voice deliberately even. 'It sounded like a bit of fun after the last six months you've had out there. Is there any reason you wouldn't want to go?'

She hesitated a fraction too long. 'No.'

'Okay.' He smiled carefully. 'So, what's the issue?'

Fliss lowered her bergen, clearly buying herself time. 'I thought tonight was about...' She flushed. 'I don't *know* what it's about. Talking, or...sex, I guess.'

He deliberately didn't react. He couldn't say the same for his body.

'You weren't planning to eat?'

'I...obviously.'

She didn't fool him; she clearly hadn't considered food at all. He suspected she'd been so caught up in doing something out of character that she'd only geared herself up for the moment itself, without thinking around it.

In a sense it was flattering.

'You just thought we'd go to the room and get down to it?' he continued, not unkindly.

'Well...no.'

'How exactly did you think the evening would pan out, Fliss?'

'I don't know but I...we were going to...sleep together...the other day,' she croaked eventually.

'For the record, there wasn't going to be any sleeping going on.' He arched his eyebrows.

She shivered in appreciation. 'No.'

'But at least then it would have been spontaneous. Natural,' he pointed out. 'This isn't the same. I just thought it would be nice to go for a meal together, chat a little, let things develop at their own pace.'

She paused. He was throwing her off, one minute firing her up and the next trying to relax her. She wasn't sure if it was deliberate, or if Ash himself was having trouble deciding which he'd rather do.

'That does sound…nice. But why go out? The restaurant has a good reputation.'

'And it's also too close to the bedrooms. Do you really think you'd be able to relax? I felt it would help to get right away from here for a few hours, release the pressure valve and just get to know each other a little.'

Not entirely a lie.

'Is that what you usually do? Get to know your one-night stands?'

'I've told you before, you shouldn't go on reputation alone. Yes, I like to know a little about a woman I might choose to have sex with. And, even if I didn't, I'd like to know a little about *you.*'

He let her digest that for a moment, wondering if it would frighten her off. He already knew enough to know that talking about herself was the last thing she enjoyed doing.

She sucked in a steadying breath, her words slow and thoughtful.

'You're talking about a meal and an evening out?'

'Yes.'

'Kind of like a date?'

'Exactly like a date.'

'Okay, then.' Fliss offered him a weak smile just as the lift stopped and the doors *pinged* open.

Rucksacks in hand, they walked along the corridor together.

'Fine, then how about I meet you in the lobby, say around nineteen-hundred hours?'

'Nineteen-hundred hours.' She nodded as she stopped at a bedroom door. 'This is me.'

Obligingly, he set her kit down and as he stood outside her door he debated the wisdom of his decision to wait. It took a dignified effort to continue along the corridor.

A linen closet separated his room from hers.

Slipping his keycard out of his pocket, Ash deftly passed it through the lock, opening the door before he could change his mind. But in his peripheral vision he could see Fliss still stuck at her own door, stabbing the card into the reader. He watched it flash red a couple of times. Pushing his door open, he dropped his bergens inside and strode back down the corridor to take the keycard gently from her fingers.

'Don't be so rushed,' he murmured, sliding it gracefully through the lock and seeing the green light. Like some kind of sign. 'Take it slowly.'

'Slowly,' she echoed shakily. 'Got it.'

They both knew they were talking about more than the lock.

'You're sure you're not coming in?' Tentatively, she raised one hand to touch his lapel with her palm.

He knew it was her attempt to avoid having to go to the carnival, but it still had an effect. He groaned. His self-control was barely intact as it was.

'Fliss, I'm trying to do the gentlemanly thing here.'

'I never asked for that,' she whispered. 'It wasn't the gentle side of you which attracted me in the first place.'

'You wouldn't like the other side of me,' he growled.

'How do you know?'

They stood, unmoving and silent, until she snatched back her hand, yanked at the door handle and stumbled over the threshold.

'Never mind. You're right. I'm not exactly

the kind of woman who elicits impulsive tendencies.'

He followed her in swiftly, catching her shoulders and spinning her back around as he drew her close.

'That's where you're wrong.'

His hands cupping her face, he pinned her back against the wall and lowered his mouth to hers. She tasted every bit as sweet as he recalled, but this time it was laced with a hint of ferocity, as though heightened by the frustration of their last encounter. He caught her lower lip in his as her hands inched up his arms to rest on his shoulders, her body moulding itself to his despite the uniforms in the way.

This needed to stop. It wasn't the way he wanted things to go between them.

She flicked her tongue over his.

With another groan Ash deepened the kiss, so long and deep that his only thought was that he could drown in her kisses and never want to come up for air. Heat licking over him, his hands glided up her body to rest at the underside of her breasts. He wanted to touch every incredible inch of her body, and have her touch every single inch of his.

As abruptly as he'd started it, Ash drew away, his voice rasping. '*Now* do you see that you're the kind of woman who can drive a man wild with longing?'

Without another word, he hauled open the door and marched to his own room before temptation undermined him.

Closing the door, he leaned heavily on it.

This was no longer just a matter of a distraction from the blackness inside him. Or about getting past Fliss's prickly armour. It was more than that. It had become a matter of exerting his own self-control. He wanted her with a need that actually scared him.

He couldn't allow his emotions to rule him like that. If he could control the course of the evening, rein in his hunger for Fliss long enough to get through a date, then enjoy one incredible night with the woman before walking away and never looking back, then maybe he could indulge in his desire for her without losing his prized self-control.

He had to. If he didn't, then stirring *any* emotions tonight could bring the whole lot crashing down.

CHAPTER SEVEN

FLISS SCREWED CLOSED the lid of her new mascara bottle with shaking hands as she checked her reflection in the mirror with a hesitant smile and tried to quell the rolling in her lower abdomen. An orchestra of crickets might as well have decamped in there. She rarely wore makeup, certainly never at work, but she'd found a few perfect supplies at the local market—not too much, but enough to enhance her sunkissed glow—and couldn't help wondering if Ash would like what he saw.

Logically, it shouldn't matter; she'd learned a long time ago not to care what anyone thought. But nothing about Ash was what she was used to. Logic seemed to fly out of the window when he was around, as did practicality. She should have refused the moment he'd raised the idea of seeing the carnival. After the last couple of emotional weeks, it threatened to unearth things best left forgotten. Instead, she'd let Ash talk her into it.

She was acting on pure lust and complete gut instinct. It was absurd and it was terrifying.

And it was also intoxicating.

She couldn't even remember when she'd last been excited about going on a date, let alone excited about getting *ready* to go on a date. She'd heard girls giggling about it over the years, but she'd never understood it. Until now. It was why she'd actually enjoyed spending a portion of her afternoon, when she would otherwise have preferred to be sleeping, going down to the local tourist market and uncovering unexpected treasures like the tiny pot of powder and brush, the subtly sparkling lipgloss and the wand of mascara. She'd even managed to squeeze in an appointment at the hotel's hair salon. Elle would never have recognised her, but she could hear her friend's approving voice in her ear, urging Fliss to just have fun for once.

Well, she definitely intended to do that.

Satisfied, she reached for her keycard and new clutch bag and then for the door handle.

It was ten to seven and she was going to be early—dating rules probably dictated that she shouldn't be, but Fliss couldn't help that. Punctuality was ingrained in her. She couldn't change that now.

Taking every last ounce of confidence in her hands, she stepped out of the door and made her way to the lift. The last person she expected to see standing there was Ash, a crisp shirt doing little to conceal those broad shoulders or honed physique which had already marked him out as an eligible male within a contingent of the females down here. Somehow he managed to appear even more powerful and commanding than he did in his military uniform.

A hint of possessiveness shot through her, mingled with a pinch of smugness that *she* was the woman he was waiting for. But then her heart plummeted; he didn't exactly look pleased to see her hurrying straight over to his corner.

Served her right for her hubris.

'You're early too.' She nervously smoothed down her black jersey trousers to hide her unease.

The trousers might have been old but they were also comfy, flowing prettily around her legs. The perfect foil to her new, uncharacteristically sexy, cleavage-revealing halter-top, which she was suddenly thinking might be a little too nightclub for her.

'Felicity—' he looked genuinely thrown '—you look…incredible.'

With a start, Fliss realised that he hadn't immediately recognised her, but now he had he treated her to a full, very heated appraisal, darkened eyes taking in the visual of head to toe, and *everything* in between.

Her confidence bounced back a little. He

clearly liked what he saw but, when he hadn't appreciated it was her, he hadn't been about to flirt with the stranger heading in his direction. The crackle of crickets leapt around Fliss even more madly.

'Your hair,' he managed.

Self-consciously, she flicked at the cascade of gold, expertly volumised so that she felt like some kind of glamorous shampoo model.

'New clothes?'

Her confidence rose a little higher again. He was having a hard time lifting his eyes from her cleavage. But, rather than feeling self-conscious, or condemning Ash for his primal reaction, an unexpected sliver of sensual power rippled through her. She felt bold and sexy, and proudly feminine. She chose not to answer the question.

'Shall we see if the taxi is here?'

He stepped close to her by way of response, sliding a strong palm to the dip of her back as they moved through the foyer. It was such a small but intimate gesture, he might as well have seared its impression into her skin.

'Are you hungry?' he murmured into her hair.

Stay calm.

'Famished.'

'Good.' He guided her out of the doors and to the waiting taxi. 'Then let's go.'

* * *

The drive was fortunately short—being so close to Ash on the back seat was having a woeful effect on her ability to breathe, let alone to construct coherent sentences. She tried to move her thigh from his, the solid, muscular length playing havoc on her senses, but he simply closed the gap again and all she could think about was what was going to happen later that evening back in the hotel room.

Arriving at their destination was both a relief and a disappointment and Fliss tried to concentrate on the carnival sounds to distract herself. The evening had barely started and she was already hung up on what was to come. She was beginning to be grateful to Ash for starting the evening far away from the hotel.

The driver had already warned them that the main town was closed to traffic for the parade so they would have to continue the rest of the way on foot. They trailed along cobbled streets with old buildings built with yellow and cream stone and red-tiled roofs. Flowers and streamers hung from windows of various homes and shops.

Yet, even as they got closer to the central square, and the sounds of music and laughter grew louder, Fliss still wasn't prepared for turning the corner into the main parade street.

It swept her away in an instant.

More flowers, flags, streamers and lanterns adorned the wide road in their hundreds—as far as the eye could see. Laughing couples and families thronged the place, and live music played as people danced in the street. Now and then, incredible cooking smells wafted to her nostrils, making her stomach rumble in appreciation.

Ash turned his head to look at her and she grinned, unabashed. Then, his arm firmly around her shoulders and her body melded to his, he led her into the crowds.

'Where are we heading?' she said, laughing.

He smiled, shaking his head to indicate he hadn't heard her over the bustling street.

'Say again?'

'Where are we heading?'

'Anywhere we want.' Ash placed his lips to her ear, so close his breath tickled her. 'Stop me if you see anywhere which takes your fancy.'

She didn't want to draw comparisons. What good would it do? Still, it felt heady to be so impromptu. Dates in previous relationships had been so planned, so rigid—everything she'd thought she wanted. She was beginning to realise that predictability could be dull and uninspiring.

Except this wasn't really a date and it certainly wasn't the start of a relationship. She needed to remember that.

'Here.' She stopped Ash abruptly.

A small but pretty restaurant had caught her eye. Unlike some of the other places, with tables spilling out into the road and smiling servers running around a multitude of tourists, this place looked smaller, more family-run. And there looked to be several locals enjoying a meal, which was always a good sign in Fliss's book.

'Good choice,' Ash agreed, threading his way to a table for two and holding her chair out for her to sit down, before seating himself at ninety degrees.

It was nicer than sitting opposite him, Fliss thought with surprise, and it allowed them both to watch the festival without the pressure to make conversation. He was making everything so easy; if only she could convince her over-excited body to agree.

With a concerted effort, Fliss pushed her nerves about the later part of the evening to the back of her mind and focused on the carnival around them. The bands had taken a break and the dancing had stopped but she could still hear plenty of buzz, and music in the distance. Craning her neck eagerly, she realised that the parade had begun and the first troubadours and baton-twirlers were moving energetically down the streets, leading the most breathtaking floats Fliss had ever seen.

She clapped her hands along with the crowd, their appreciation evident. This wasn't going to be such a tense evening, after all.

It was an hour before the last of the floats passed by, the music slowly drifting away, the lanterns now casting a warm glow over the darkening sky. Ash watched as Fliss turned back, her whole body more relaxed than he'd seen all evening. Possibly ever.

She glanced at her empty place setting.

'The meal's gone?'

'You finished it.' He chuckled softly. 'You don't remember?'

She offered a rueful smile. 'I know I'm full, and I know the food was beautiful.' She glanced at the bottle of red wine. 'Ah, well, that isn't why I'm feeling so chilled out; it's only half empty.'

He didn't have the heart to tell her it was their second bottle and she'd drank two-thirds of that one.

They fell into an easy silence, the street scene still offering plenty of entertainment.

'So you enjoyed the parade?' Ash asked, once the waiter had brought them a round of coffees.

'I loved it.' She nodded, her eyes sparkling happily. 'It was almost magical. And now all the lanterns are so pretty; it's like being in a fairy tale.'

'I'm glad you had fun.' He was careful to keep his tone upbeat. 'I still can't believe you've never been to a festival.'

He watched Fliss's mind ticking over, wondering how best to respond. But then the server chose that moment to clear the dishes from their table and by the time they were alone again Ash feared she might have composed herself enough to brush him off. He was surprised when she answered hesitantly.

'It wasn't somewhere my uncle wanted to take me.'

'He didn't want to, or you didn't wan'

She slowly stirred her coffee, her e on the mini-vortex.

'A bit of both, probably.'

He waited quietly in the more of her own volit that ate away at A better, to understan him out. He couldn't ex him so much.

Then again, she wasn't shooting him down either. It could mean part of her wanted to talk, if he could just coax it out of her without scaring her off.

'You said your uncle raised you?'

She paused, then nodded. 'From the age of eight.'

'You mentioned your mother wasn't kind to you.'

Perhaps by reminding her of things she'd already told him, it would help her to feel she'd already trusted him once. At least partially.

A brittle sound escaped her. 'I represented the end of all her dreams. And she never let me forget it.'

He'd seen that often enough, with other kids in care.

'She was an aspiring ballerina.' Fliss bunched her shoulders.

Ah. Not that it excused it, but it gave him a better understanding of what Fliss had dealt with.

'Would she have made it?'

'I honestly don't think she would.' Fliss met his gaze, not spiteful but factual. 'My uncle said she was good, but there are thousands of *good* ones. She wasn't great, certainly not standout. She could never accept that. She always had to be someone to blame. Never herself.

Before I came along she blamed her parents for not supporting her enough. Then when she fell pregnant and neither of my two potential fathers wanted to know, that was their fault. And finally, when I came along, I was the excuse she needed to explain why she'd given up dancing altogether. She could be…cruel.'

'Is that why you're so responsible? So rule-abiding? Except for when you're leaping off helicopters to save injured soldiers, that is.'

'I don't know.' Fliss looked surprised. 'I've never really thought about it, I guess. I just know I vowed to myself I'd never be like my mother.'

'And yet your uncle, the General, he's one of the most responsible, straight-down-the-line men I know.'

'Yes.' A fond smile leapt to her lips. 'He was the typically duty-bound older brother. He had a younger brother who died as a baby—cot death, I think. When my mother came along within the year—another new baby and a girl to boot—I think my grandparents were overly protective.'

'So, as she grew up, your mother got away with a lot?'

'If you listen to her then no; her father was a military man too, and she bemoans the fact they were suffocating in their strictness. But if you ask my uncle, he'll say she was given a lot of leeway. Yet the more she got, the more she demanded. She became known as a bit of a whinger, whilst my uncle was always expected to be the big brother and pick up the slack. He carried that with him when he followed in my grandfather's footsteps into the Army. It's what's made him the General, I suppose.'

'And you're like him. Always striving to do the right thing,' Ash mused.

He was certainly beginning to understand her better. He and Fliss had more in common than he would have believed.

'But it doesn't make you boring, or dull.'

'I just think I was looking for someone I could trust. A man with the same qualities I see in my uncle. But I couldn't love them the way they deserved to be loved. That isn't me. I confused solid and reliable with boring and disconnected.'

'Why? Why are you so afraid to let go, Fliss?'

She offered a helpless shrug. 'I don't want to be like my mother. She only thought about herself, about what *she* wanted. Did I tell you that we didn't start off alone? That she only dragged me away from my grandparents' house when I was four? And that was because she wanted to push me into all the dancing lessons she wished that she had taken, but her parents hadn't allowed her to?'

Ash shook his head. 'Did you like dancing?'

'I *hated* dancing. But she said I was being selfish. That I owed her that much. I'd taken away her dream of dancing, so the least I could do was try to be half the dancer she felt she had been. It took my uncle four years to track us down. We were squatting in a house with about twenty others. We had no heating, no food because all the money she had went on sparkling new dresses so she could push me onto the circuit.'

He'd seen and heard a little about pageants over the years.

'They can be quite cut-throat, can't they.'

'That's an understatement.'

He could virtually see the nausea, the fear rising in her.

'So you loathed it,' he confirmed.

She bounced her head, unable to answer him for a moment. 'Every single second of the humiliation. My mother would scream and bawl at me for missing a pivot or split. I was five, Ash. *Five.* I should have been playing on the swings, or being taught how to ride a bike. Having fun, laughing. Being loved.'

His throat constricted. He knew exactly how that felt. The loneliness, the despair, the rejection.

'My uncle found us backstage after one of

those competitions. I was on the floor, sobbing over something or other, when he walked in and I thought he looked like the biggest, bravest, most heroic man I'd ever seen.'

'That was when he gave her the ultimatum.' Ash drew his lips into a thin line.

She stopped abruptly, dropping her eyes from his, but he could see that, even now, her pain was still as intense.

'Fliss?'

'When my mother refused to leave with him—' her voice dropped to a whisper '—she told him I was useless anyway and that she was better off without me. Then she dragged me off the floor and threw me across the room to him. She told him if he wanted to look after a worthless baby like me, then he could have me. Finally she walked out.'

Anger rushed up inside of Ash, along with something else. A fierce protectiveness. A need to ensure that no one hurt her or made her feel so worthless ever again.

He knew it wasn't his place to feel that way but he couldn't curb it; it refused to be pushed aside.

'Ash, I don't want to talk about this any more.'

Nodding grimly, Ash pulled his wallet out and thrust a generous pile of notes at the delighted server and pulled Fliss gently from her chair. Right now, she needed to be reminded of the better side of life. And he was determined to be the one to do that for her.

'Come on, Fliss. Time to get out of here.'

CHAPTER EIGHT

'WHERE ARE WE GOING?' Fliss cried as he clasped her hand, holding her tightly as he weaved his way through the crowds, the music and dancing starting up once again to their left as they were jostled and bumped by revellers.

Holding on as though he never wanted to let her go, Ash maintained the pace and, although she was initially reluctant, Fliss discovered the further they got from the restaurant, the more she felt as though she was leaving the conversation—and her past—behind.

The only time Ash stopped was when they passed a street vendor selling popcorn. He halted abruptly but, instead of buying a cone of hot buttered puffs, he asked for a small bag of kernels.

'What are they for?' she asked curiously.

Dropping them inside his shirt pocket, he patted the outside, his expression giving nothing away.

'Secret.'

And then, before she had a chance to say

anything more, he set off again, her hand still tightly in his, and resumed their determined pace. By the time he pulled them both left into a side street that was decidedly less packed than the main route, Fliss had forgotten her earlier unease and felt a renewed sense of adventure. She marvelled at the effect. How easy Ash made it for her.

'According to our server, there's a path up the hillside here which offers a view out over the town. Apparently it's well worth a look.'

'I never even heard you ask.'

He shot her an indulgent smile which lifted her spirits even further.

'That's because you were too entranced by the floats. So, are you up for it?'

She glanced up at the cobbled path, infrequent lanterns offering pinpoints of light, lending it an almost romantic air.

'Sure, why not?'

As they headed along the narrowing streets, she couldn't suppress the rush of pleasure that, even though they were no longer pushing through crowds, he still enveloped her hand in his as though he wasn't ready to let her go.

As they left the last of the bars and restaurants, souvenir shops and revellers behind, the night closed around them like their own personal cloak. The path climbed steadily, a stone wall protecting them from the ever-increasing drop on one side whilst higgledy-piggledy stone buildings lined the other.

As the space between the festival lanterns stretched longer and longer, they began to pass the occasional couple, kissing passionately as they leaned on the wall or up against the buildings, cocooned in their own little world and oblivious to Ash and Fliss approaching. Yet another reminder of a typical carefree youth which Fliss had never allowed herself to experience.

Partly because she was afraid of becoming her mother and having a baby, only to make the child's life the same misery Fliss herself had endured. But also partly, Fliss was loathed to admit, because she was so prickly that no boy had ever wanted her enough—or, at least, made her *feel* wanted enough—to let go of her tightly held reins to try.

'This must be it.' Ash broke into her musings. 'So, what do you make of it?'

Peering around his shoulder as they turned to their left, Fliss took in the view and gasped.

The town beneath them seemed to be dotted by a thousand pretty fairy lights, the floats strategically sited around the streets for festival-goers to enjoy. It was prettier than she could have imag-

ined. She moved to the parapet and stood trans-
fixed, unable to articulate how she felt.

'You seem tense. It was all those couples kissing, wasn't it?' he asked, coming to stand next
to her but deliberately giving her a little space.

She turned to look at him, confused.

'I'm not uncomfortable. If anything, I confess
I might have felt a little…envious. Fusty Fliss,
too uptight for anything like that.'

She snapped her mouth shut, wishing she
hadn't said that. She certainly wasn't about to
tell him where it had come from.

'*Fusty?* Is that so?' Ash muttered, angling his
body so he was now facing her, looking straight
into her eyes as though he could see every last
worry etched in her face. 'Only *I* don't think
that's entirely true.'

Ash lifted his hands to her shoulders, compelling her to turn her body, only to pull it against
his, unbelievably hard and unyielding. Her insides turned to molten liquid.

She wanted him with an ache so fierce it
should have frightened her.

He dipped his head to skim her lips with his
own. He drew a lazy line across her bottom
lip with his tongue. He slid his tongue in just
enough to tease her. And all the while she could
only cling to him, unable to tell whether he was
the one thing stopping her from going under

or the one thing pulling her beneath the sensual waves. Finally, Ash lifted her arms to hook them around his neck, allowing him greater access to the rest of her body, and she didn't stop him. She couldn't.

His hands explored her body, tracing every contour, firing every nerve-ending. Fliss opened her mouth to invite him further inside and he complied. Tasting her, teasing her. She pressed her body harder against his, the solid length of his erection unmistakable between them. It was a turn-on to know just how much he wanted her and instinctively she rocked against him.

He made a low, guttural sound in the back of his throat. Nerves and boldness mingled and Fliss rocked against him again.

'Be careful,' he warned her.

'What if I don't want to be?' she whispered back shakily.

He stilled, pulling back from her so he could look her in the eye. 'Don't you?'

She hesitated before offering a helpless shrug. 'I don't know.'

She wanted to do something out of character, go a little crazy. But she'd been trapped by her own set of unbending rules for so long that she didn't know how to break free.

'Do you trust me?' he demanded gruffly.

She thought back to the soldier she'd spoken

to out in the field. The way every man who had worked with Ash only had good things to say about him.

'Yes,' she murmured.

He gave a curt, almost imperceptible nod, then leaned in to resume their kissing. But this time it was different. So intense and passionate her toes actually curled with pleasure. She ran her hands languidly over his body, exploring the taut, bunched muscles of his shoulders, his back, his obliques. Every inch of him was honed and uncompromising, without an inch of soft skin. And for tonight it was all hers. She only wished she knew exactly what to do with him.

It had never been like this in the past. The physical side of her limited relationships had been pleasant enough, if a little perfunctory. But nothing about Ash was *pleasant.* He was powerful, thrilling, dangerous. Fliss could imagine sex with him wouldn't be any less so. She just needed to convince him that she was ready for him to stop holding back. She let her hands drop to his backside, slipping her fingers in the pockets and hesitantly pulling him tighter against her.

As if reading her thoughts, Ash pressed her against the wall. With one knee, he nudged her legs apart and slid a steel-like thigh against the heat there. His lips blazed a sizzling trail all the way down the sensitive cord of her neck so that she couldn't help but dip her head to the side with a soft sigh, her hands barely holding onto his body as weakness trickled into her limbs.

Every part of her body was coming alive under his touch. He made her feel wanted. Needed. She arched her body towards him in subconscious invitation.

Dropping a hand lazily over her breasts, over nipples aching to be touched, Ash circled her ribcage, his strong hands and fingers splayed over her skin making her feel dainty and feminine. Then he flicked a thumb up and over the aching bud, his kisses dipping into the hollow at the base of her neck. Gasping, Fliss snapped her head back up.

'Ash...'

She didn't want him to stop but she couldn't help her reaction. Her well-worn shackles of propriety had reasserted themselves, making her feel constrained and awkward. They were so much more exposed up here than they had been in the camp—in more ways than one.

'Shh, I promise you that no one's around,' he murmured. 'No one can see us, or hear us.'

She wished she didn't care. They were only kissing, for pity's sake. Why couldn't she be caught up in their little bubble, just as those few couples they had passed on the way up had been?

'You didn't seem this uncomfortable between the shipping containers and tents back at camp,' he pointed out gently.

'I was more comfortable there,' she hedged. 'It was familiar. Elle and I sunbathed there a few times—in rare moments of down-time, that is—and no one had ever stumbled on us before. Plus, it happened so fast, I didn't have time to second-guess myself.'

'Do you want to stop?'

There was no censure in his tone, no accusation, just a simple question. He wasn't trying to push her faster than she was prepared to go, although Fliss could tell how passionately he wanted her. A shiver of delight cascaded through her.

'I don't want to stop,' she realised aloud. She just needed reassurance.

'Shh, listen,' he told her. 'Close your eyes and listen.'

Obediently, she did.

'What am I listening for?' she asked after a moment, opening her eyes again. 'Aside from the faint sounds of the parade below, I can't hear anything.'

It was still and silent and, with the last lanterns much further down the path, the only light was the glow from the stars, and their eyes had long since adjusted to that.

'Precisely.'

She could hear the smile in his voice.

Feeling more secure, Fliss looped her arms around Ash's neck and pressed her lips to his. They both knew he could have made her forget all her concerns with that clever mouth of his. The fact that he'd chosen to be patient and let her feel comfortable in her own time spoke volumes.

'Happier?' he murmured against her mouth in amusement.

'Much.' She smiled at him, still not lifting her lips from his.

They kissed as he reached up to take one of her hands in his, strong fingers curling around hers. They kissed as he held both their hands to her chest, as though they might be slow dancing. They kissed as she felt her heart beating rhythmically against her fingers. Her body hummed with contentment but, more importantly in that instant, her heart did too. It felt so right, and so natural.

Breathing in, Fliss allowed herself to imagine what it would be like to have this kind of lust and excitement every day. It wasn't what this one night was about with Ash, she knew that, but it made her think that maybe the life she'd been trying to create for herself had never worked out because it wasn't right. She imagined what it might be like to stop trying to convince herself that she was in love with men like Robert, and just allowed herself to fall for a man like Ash. She imagined that could be such a very easy thing to do.

And then Fliss stopped imagining altogether. Finally giving in to what her body was trying to tell her, and losing herself in the magic Ash was conjuring throughout her body.

She dropped her hand down between their bodies and let her knuckles graze the hard length of his erection through the fabric of his trousers. His reaction was immediate, and unmistakable.

'Fliss,' he groaned, 'I can only resist so much.'

'So don't resist,' she whispered, loving the way his voice sounded so torn. So raw.

For a fraction of a second he hesitated, and then he acted. His hand skimmed over her ribcage, the bare sliver of skin of her lower abdomen, the loose waistband of her pants. She sucked in a breath, anticipating his next move, longing for it. Finally, he dipped his fingers beneath the material.

He hadn't planned on anything happening out here. Certainly not like this. He'd genuinely brought her up here because he'd thought it would be pretty and romantic. But then she'd told him how envious she was of the uninhibited displays of the few young couples in love who they'd passed on the way up, and he'd wanted to release that dormant side of her, the passion he knew lurked so close to the surface but which she didn't believe existed.

Now he found himself consumed with his own lust, and a need to see her come undone in his arms.

She was like a drug to him. He wanted her with an intensity which shook him, had done ever since that moment in the supply room in camp. He wanted her with a ferocity he didn't recognise. Driven, as if he was on some kind of mission.

Tonight was his one night to sate this insatiable hunger he seemed to have for Fliss.

Not for the first time, Ash slammed away the question of whether one night would ever be enough with this woman. He couldn't afford to think that way. One night would *have* to be enough; it was all they had. And then it would be back to their careers, heads down and eyes in, that they had both worked at for so long. Neither of them could afford to let anyone else close, to create distractions, to get hurt.

He almost held his breath as he grazed his fingers lower, deliciously hot and damp through the flimsiest scrap of lacy fabric. She moaned and moved against his hand, urging him on, and Ash barely clung onto his self-control. He drew his body back so that he could see her in the starlight. She met his gaze, her eyes wide and dark, biting her lip as she waited for him to touch her just where she needed him. Her expression was pure, instinctual desire and he revelled in the proud sensation of being the one to put it there.

His eyes never leaving her face, he slid his finger under the lace. She made a small sound, clearly fighting to keep her gaze locked with his as she opened her legs a fraction wider. It was all the invitation Ash needed.

He let her move her hands back up his body before dipping his head to kiss her neck the way she'd loved earlier, all the while moving his fingers back and forth, unhurried at first, grazing their mark with deliberate precision. Her fingers bit into his shoulders as she tried to shift against his hand but he moved it away, only returning it when she stopped.

'Wicked,' she breathed into the night air and his slow smile curved into her skin as he sought out the nub of her sex, her gasp only tightening his own body all the more.

He moved quicker this time, the slickness of her threatening every inch of his willpower just as much as her soft sounds and low moans. At last, he slipped his finger inside her tightness, her body arching in response.

'So damned wet,' he growled, his teeth nipping gently at her neck.

Fliss moved her head to bury it into his shoulder but he reached up with his other hand and cupped her chin.

'Don't hide your head,' he commanded huskily. 'I want to watch you come.'

She trembled against him and Ash flicked his thumb over her entrance as his fingers moved inside her, the pressure making her squirm. She was so very tight and he could only imagine how she would feel around him later tonight. His movements became faster, more concentrated, watching as her eyelids grew hooded. She was close, and he wanted it to be perfect for her. Needed it to be.

She gripped his shoulders tighter, her eyes closed now, her head dropping slightly forward, and he kept moving, feeling the tension mount in her body. And then, with a low cry, she climaxed, squeezing down around his fingers then releasing, and finally pulsing around them in waves of pleasure. He waited, careful not to move his hand until she was ready for him to, all the while dropping light kisses onto her bowed head so that she felt safe.

He understood just how much it had taken for

her to confide in him the way she had this evening. In a sense, the fact that they'd both had a difficult childhood had created an additional closeness Ash hadn't been prepared for.

But this closeness is transient, he reminded himself sharply. It would be wrong of him to allow either of them to confuse a temporary moment of bonding for anything more—not to mention unfair on Fliss—just because his head was a bit of an emotional wreck right now with the funeral looming.

He needed to find the right moment to remind her—remind himself—that it was still just sex.

He was still lost in his thoughts when Fliss eventually lifted her head.

'Ash?'

He turned his head, the sight of her soothing his jostling thoughts.

Tell her now.

'You look annoyed.' She peered at him nervously, her initial euphoria seeming to disappear before his eyes.

He hesitated. He *was* annoyed, but at himself, not at Fliss. It wouldn't be fair to burst her bubble when *she* wasn't the one apparently having difficulty remembering it was just about sex. It was *him*. But giving herself to him with such abandon was so out of character for Fliss, Ash hated that her happiness was so fragile.

He hated that he could be the one to hurt her when suddenly all he wanted to do was protect her. Always.

Ridiculous. Just sex. Right?

'I'm not remotely annoyed,' he reassured her, forcing a rueful smile to his lips as he searched for a plausible distraction for his reaction. 'Frustrated, maybe.'

She flushed prettily, the way he'd become accustomed to her doing when she was feeling self-conscious. She lowered her hand down his body which, despite everything, kicked in primal need.

Just sex.

'Not here,' he growled, catching her wrist. 'I want to strip you down and taste every last inch of you before I finally slide inside you.'

'Then shall we go back to the hotel?' Her delighted smile was shy and seductive at the same time. 'We only have five hours before you have to leave for your flight.'

Deep inside Ash, something came apart. This was the confirmation he needed that he'd been imagining it when he'd thought Fliss was opening up to him as though there was more between them than just a one-night stand.

So why didn't that please him more?

'Let's go,' he answered grimly, shoving the reservations from his head.

Placing his arm protectively around her shoulders, they headed back down the hillside, her body nestling against his, a perfect fit.

Just sex.

He was finally beginning to convince himself. Still, it was going to be a painfully long taxi ride all the way back, so perhaps it was also the chance he needed to sort his head out.

CHAPTER NINE

SOMETHING WAS DIFFERENT.

Fliss's heart was beating so madly that it felt as though a jackhammer was assaulting her chest the entire journey to the hotel.

His arm might still be around her shoulders, his hard body almost glued to hers on the hot car seats, but mentally Ash was pulling away from her. And she had a fair idea why.

She'd broken their agreement.

She hadn't intended to. But there it was. She'd forgotten the *just sex* part of it and was at serious risk of falling for Ash. And he must know it. It explained why he was trying to distance himself emotionally.

She wanted to put it down to her inexperience with casual flings, but deep down she was afraid it was more than that. It wasn't the unfamiliar act of a one-night stand which was confusing her, but more the unique man sitting tantalisingly close to her. The one who had made her forget her surroundings back up on that hillside, who had made her forget all her usual rules and codes, and forget herself. When he'd played her body with such skill and finesse that it had thrummed with pleasure. When he'd peeled away the armour she'd spent decades melding for herself, and shown her how to live in that one breathtaking moment. And when he'd laced his fingers through hers and dropped a kiss on her soft knuckles as if he really cared about her.

She'd forgotten all her rules and she'd let herself imagine something more with him. But when she came back down to earth she would remember that neither of them had room in their lives for that. If she was going to salvage tonight then she needed to convince him he had misunderstood, that she wasn't really thinking with her heart instead of her head. She needed to convince him that it was only about the sex for her too.

Because the alternative was that Ash would call it a night now rather than risk any unwanted further entanglement. And Fliss suddenly suspected that no other man was ever going to get under her skin the way Ash had, and if she didn't indulge in this one night of wanton abandon with him then she would regret it for the rest of her life.

Somehow, she had to make Ash believe that she *did* actually know what she was doing.

Even if she didn't.

Suppressing her nerves, Fliss twisted her body around to his and forced herself to sound confident as she leaned in to whisper in his ear. 'This journey is taking way too long.'

'We'll be back soon.'

Ash pulled his lips into a tight line, but Fliss was determined not to be dismissed. She dipped her head so that her lips were skimming the soft dip by his ear.

'Not soon enough,' she murmured, deliberately letting one hand drop onto his thigh. High enough that her desire was clear, but low enough so that it would pique his interest.

At least, she hoped it would. This was about heightening the sexual intensity, but they both knew she wasn't about to do anything else in the back seat of a taxi. Fliss suddenly wished she was a little more skilled in the bedroom department. She walked her fingers a torturously slow inch higher, her voice still a whisper.

'I can hardly wait to touch you properly.'

He caught her wrist in his strong fingers, just as he had on the hilltop, stopping it from moving any higher. But at least he didn't cast her away. In fact, the wall between them was beginning to crumble again. Fliss felt a punch of triumph. She'd convinced Ash that she was only thinking about the sex. And the funny thing about it was that, in the process, she'd started to convince herself that she felt that way too.

'I'm not made of stone, Felicity,' he warned. His voice was a low, strained rumble which seemed to burrow into her lower abdomen. She swallowed.

'I'm not asking you to be.'

Trusting her to keep her hand where it was, he let go and cupped her jaw, forcing her to look at him. For several long moments they held each other's eyes wordlessly. Her stomach flip-flopped. Ash's gaze was so intense it was almost black with desire, allaying any fears that he didn't want her any more. The realisation boosted her confidence more than any words could have.

Closing the gap between them, Fliss pressed her lips to his, so demanding and urgent she barely recognised herself. But she liked it. She liked the boldness Ash brought out in her, and she loved the way his resistance barely lasted a second before he was kissing her back with such heat she could hardly breathe.

She couldn't stop herself any longer. She cupped him through his trousers and he reacted instantly. Lust shot through her and her body arched towards his as liquid desire pooled at her core. If it hadn't been for the driver she didn't think she could have stopped herself from taking it further.

Her. Felicity Delaunay.

'I need more,' she moaned softly.

He pulled at her lower lip with his teeth, gently teasing her, his thumb grazing up and down her jawline.

'Soon,' Ash muttered, without lifting his head. 'I promise.'

Every last drop of their mutual desire was expressed in that kiss. Constrained to that kiss. First shallow and fast, then deepening and slowing. His mouth explored hers just as he had before, yet every stroke of his tongue and pass of his lips ignited new flames throughout Fliss's body as she revelled in the intoxicating feel of his mouth.

It was almost a relief when the taxi finally drew up outside the hotel and they tumbled out, barely able to conceal their hurry. Fliss felt momentarily bereft as Ash paused to pay the driver, but then he snaked his arm around her waist as he swept them inside the hotel lobby and across to the lifts. The wait felt interminably long.

Finally they ducked inside and stood, eyes fixed ahead, just waiting for the doors to close so that they could resume the kiss where they'd left off in the taxi. Her self-control was in tatters and her body throbbed. Finally, mercifully, the doors began to slide closed and Fliss was just imagining Ash hauling her up against the walls of the lift when a walking stick was jammed through the rapidly closing gap.

She felt Ash tug her gently to the side as the doors *pinged* open and an elderly couple shuffled inside, smiling kindly at them.

'Lovely evening.'

'Lovely,' Ash agreed, his voice admirably clear. 'Which floor?'

Her own throat tight, Fliss tried to force a smile to her lips instead. For years she'd wondered what it must feel like when other kids had lamented sneaking a boyfriend to their bedroom only for a parent to walk in. She suspected it felt a little like she was feeling now.

'Fifth floor, please.'

The same as theirs.

Fliss didn't dare glance at Ash. She felt as though she was trapped in some kind of farce and she'd never felt so overwhelmed by frustrated longing before. Just another tiny detail which set the night apart from any other she'd ever experienced.

The lift sped upwards. The silence almost cloying, though no one else appeared to notice.

'Have you been enjoying yourselves?'

A gurgle of laughter bubbled up inside Fliss.

Only Ash's arm, offering her silent support, allowed her to control it.

'Very pleasant, thank you,' he responded politely. 'The carnival in the local town was particularly impressive. Have you seen it?'

Smooth and polite, she was impressed. Her own brain was barely functioning it was so overcome with lust. As the couple enthused about the carnival, Fliss fought to regain some semblance of self-control. It was only when the lift reached their floor and the couple stepped out at a snail's pace that the giggle bubbled up again.

Her shoulders shook with smothered laughter as she and Ash kept back. Even his unruffled air didn't help her. How could he be so unconcerned when she felt so on edge? It didn't help that she didn't know what they were supposed to do now. Go to his room? Go to hers? Each go to their own?

It was only when the elderly pair stopped next to her room, fumbling with the keycard with only a fraction less dexterity than Fliss herself had displayed earlier, that Ash broke contact with her to go to their aid, unlocking their door with ease and shrugging off their gushing thanks as he held the door open whilst they shuffled inside.

Uncertain of herself, Fliss lurched to her own

bedroom door and tried to retrieve her card from her purse, her fumbling hands hampering her efforts.

'My room,' Ash muttered, startling her as he grabbed her hand and tugged her past the linen cupboard and to his own door, deftly opening it and hauling her inside. 'Your headboard backs right onto their wall.'

As the door closed behind them, Fliss finally let go of the mildly hysterical laugh she'd been suppressing. It took her a few moments before she realised, to her surprise, that Ash was laughing too. Their eyes locked for a moment, only making them laugh all the more. As he sank onto the edge of the bed, Fliss leaned on the wall, letting the moment of humour release some pent-up tension.

'We couldn't have timed that any worse,' Ash joked, eventually sobering up.

'I know.' She shook her head. 'But I didn't think you were bothered.'

'Are you kidding? I felt like a frustrated teenager all over again.'

She bit her lip in disbelief. 'I thought it was just me.'

He shot her an arch look.

'It definitely wasn't just you. I'm just glad I have more self-control than I had as a teenager.'

'Well, you certainly have that.'

'Barely, where you're concerned.' His husky voice fired her body up in a flash. The earlier heat couldn't course through her veins fast enough, and then he reached out a hand to her.

'Come here.'

She was only too happy to comply as he hooked his fingers into her waistband and pulled her to him. His fingers skimmed up her body and, before she realised what was happening, he had undone the tie at the back of her neck and the halter-neck had dropped down to reveal her bare breasts.

'Perfect,' he breathed reverently, cupping them with his hands. 'Just as I imagined.'

She gasped as he leaned forward to draw one taut peak into his mouth. Exquisite torture. Her entire body felt as if it were on fire for him. But there was something else too. The moment of levity had created another thread between them, and they both knew it.

Just sex, remember? Fliss berated herself as she wound her fingers through his hair, instinctively letting her head fall back as she pushed her aching nipple against his skilful tongue.

Her heart gave another kick as he settled her on his lap, one leg either side, her knees resting on the bed. He was nestled perfectly between her legs, his erection straining against the fabric towards her, making her feel sexy and powerful. Suddenly, she was gripped by the impulse to take charge. To pleasure him. To make Ash spin out of control for her, the same way she had for him back on the hillside.

'You've had your fun,' she croaked. 'Now I'm having some.'

Catching him off guard, she pushed him back on the bed and concentrated on divesting Ash of his shirt.

'You're telling me you weren't already?' he challenged smugly.

Her heart raced. Feeling all fingers and thumbs, she grappled awkwardly with the buttons. She needed to distract him before he noticed.

'A different kind of fun.' She used her best seductive tone before leaning down to brush her lips against his, deliberately grazing his shirt-clad chest with her nipples.

Ash's eyes dilated with desire and she felt another kick of adrenalin. She doubted he let many women take charge over him.

Finally, to her relief, the last fastening slid from its soft anchorage and she pushed the garment off his broad shoulders, which she'd hungered to touch like this ever since that day in the supply room. Fliss lowered her body again to taste his mouth with hers, revelling in the sensation of her nipples grazing over the smattering of hair on his bare chest. His erection twitched against her again, almost making her forget her plan.

Almost.

She rained tiny kisses down on his lips, his neck, his chest, following the trail her fingers blazed, his sharp intake of breath like a silent cheer to carry on. But she couldn't shake the feeling that Ash wasn't completely relaxed; he was only letting her take the lead for so long. She forced herself to take her time, inhaling the woodsy, leathery scent, gradually moving lower. *Lower.* Sliding down his body an inch at a time, over abs, his belly button, the muscular definition of his lower abdomen before it dipped below the waistband of his trousers. And all the while she traced the grenade scar with her fingers and her tongue, revelling in the fact that he didn't stop her.

She was relieved when her fingers unbuckled his belt and lowered his zip with far more ease than she'd managed his shirt. His erection strained against the soft fabric of his boxers. Hooking her fingers over the waistband, she pulled the material down and lowered her lips to kiss the silky tip, then to the side where the grenade wound had stopped mercifully short.

She'd seen enough wounded soldiers to know

that the genital area was one of the least pro-
tected areas, with no body armour to shield it.

Before Fliss knew what was happening, he
had scooped her onto the bed and flipped her
over onto her back, sliding the rest of her clothes
off with slick efficiency. She frowned uncertainly.

'Why did you stop me?'

'Because that's not how it's going to play out,'
he growled fiercely.

'Why not?' Disappointment welled inside her.
'You can't relinquish control for a moment, can
you?'

*No, he couldn't relinquish control. Not to Fliss.
Not like that.*

No one had ever had a hold over him the way
she seemed to. Even her hurt and disappointment gnawed at him. But even that one simple
question revealed that she understood him in a
way hardly anyone had ever done. And if he let
her do what she'd intended to do, let her make
him forget everything, then he was afraid she
would pull away the last of his defences and
leave him vulnerable.

Just as he had been as a young child, pushed
from care home to foster home and back again.
Totally out of his control.

'I'll make it up to you.' He shrugged, pushing away the guilt.

She looked dubious, half sitting up to reach for him again.

'How?'

'Like this,' he muttered, dropping to his knees and parting her legs to lick her in one strong stroke.

She cried out, falling back to the bed, her hips lifting up instinctively even as she called out in panic.

'Ash, this isn't… I don't…'

'You do now.'

He heard the primitive growl in his voice moments before he buried his head in her heat. Her hips bucked against him.

Hot. Sweet. *His.*

He wanted to be the only man who had ever been able to satisfy her the way he did. Ash fought the feeling of possessiveness which stabbed through him at the idea of her with anyone else. This wasn't about anything lasting; why was he still finding it so hard to remember that?

Sliding a hand beneath her bottom to lock her in place, he raised his hand to caress one swollen breast and lowered his head again, feeling her fingers locking into his own hair as he kissed, and licked, and sucked. Her increasing moans and gasps urged him on, the way she cried out his name stoking the primal need inside him.

She was so close. He could feel her on his tongue. He slipped a finger inside, then another, marvelling at the way she stretched against him, and then he sucked on that sensitive core and pitched her over into nothingness. Her orgasm shattered over her again and again as he never let up for an instant. Her shudders finally slowed and her breathing began to even out again.

'You should have stopped,' she accused softly, only half regretfully. 'I wanted to feel you inside me.'

'Be patient,' he murmured darkly, knowing he wanted that too. Almost too much. He'd had to prove to himself he could control that searing need.

Rocking back on his heels Ash stood up, shucking off the rest of his clothes even as he reached for a condom from the bedside drawer and rolled it quickly down his length. Then he returned his mouth to where he'd left off, hearing her objection give way to a squeak of surprise as he smoothly brought her body back to simmering point.

Only then did he cover her body with his own, her breasts pillowed against his chest, her hard nipples raking his skin. She wrapped her legs instinctively around his hips, her arms snaking around his neck. He tried to hold off but she pulled him down, his tip brushing against her wet heat, intending only to ease in part way until she became accustomed to him. Without warning, she tilted her hips and tightened her legs, drawing him slickly inside with a sensual murmur.

A guttural groan filled the air and Ash didn't immediately recognise his own voice, so thick was it with desire.

'God, Fliss, I don't know how long I can last,' he warned her.

She nodded, heavy-lidded eyes fighting to open and look at him, her hands gripping his shoulders. She was already closer than he'd realised, and the knowledge pushed him perilously closer to own completion.

Think of something else. Anything.

Bracing his arms on either side of her, he forced a gap between them, allowing him to pull out of her before driving back in. Long, slow, deliberate strokes which Fliss threatened to undo when she lifted her hips and matched him, in perfect sync, all the while skimming her fingernails down his back to his buttocks, which she grasped.

'Faster,' she whispered urgently.

He wanted to take more time. He couldn't.

She was driving the pace now, meeting him stroke for stroke, and he could barely restrain himself any longer. Their combined breathing became shallower, quicker, her moans louder, her hands clutching him. He changed the angle slightly to graze her just right and immediately her body shattered around him, clamping over him then pulsing as she shuddered in his arms.

And Ash could finally let go too. He drove into her one final time as his own climax overtook him. A climax like no other before. He couldn't tell where he ended and she began. He only knew his body was exploding into hers and she was riding against him on another orgasm of her own. He heard himself call out her name and then he tipped them both over the edge.

His last thought was whether he'd ever be able to get enough of this woman.

It was only later, much later, after he'd claimed her again and again, just before the first rays of the new day started to creep over the horizon, when he realised their time was almost up and he had to leave, that Ash heard himself telling her that he was returning home for a funeral. Just those words, nothing more.

'Whose?' she asked, the concern seeping through her voice, though she was clearly trying to keep her tone even.

Just like back in the supply room, when she'd first seen the blood on his shoulder and wondered how he'd injured himself.

And, just like then, another hairline fracture cracked through his core.

'Rosie's.'

Fliss looked aghast, an angry flush discolouring her skin.

'Ash, I'm so sorry. God, how obvious. You *told* me about your foster mother; I should have remembered. I should have realised when I saw you in the hangar.'

'Don't,' he ordered, taking her hands in his and making her look him in the eye.

'You asked if I was okay and I said I was. I didn't want to talk about it. I didn't want to think about it.'

'You wanted to forget,' she realised. 'I was a distraction.'

He could lie to her. But he didn't want to; she deserved better.

'Yes.'

Instead of looking hurt or offended, however, she nodded at him with understanding. Then she fixed him with those magnificent, expressive eyes of blue and asked him if he wanted her to accompany him. Simply. Sincerely.

Another hairline crack ran through him.

He was tempted. And then he declined.

'I'm going to the funeral to show my respect, but I lost the Rosie I knew, the mother figure, years ago, and I said my goodbyes then.'

She frowned.

'I know you think that now,' she offered softly. 'But it might not feel that way when you get there. As a doctor, I've seen it a lot. Even if you've said your goodbyes, you still might not be truly prepared for the funeral.'

'I'm prepared.'

Darkness swirled and he fought against it.

'Ash, I know you have this self-control which you feel you can't let go of—' she swallowed '—even in bed with me. But you need to give yourself permission to feel any emotions which happen on the day.'

'I understand what you're saying.' He gritted his teeth. 'But I know what I'm doing. That's why I bought the popcorn.'

'Sorry?'

He had no idea why he was telling her. Part of him wanted to make her understand that he was still thinking straight, still remembering his promises to Rosie, and that grief hadn't messed up his head. Another part of him suspected he needed to tell someone. To tell *her*.

'Part of what Rosie and Wilf did was have Family Night. Movie nights, where all the foster kids would join them in the den, watch a film together and eat burgers and popcorn; games nights where we'd gather around the kitchen and play board games; baking nights, which was actually where I first learned to cook something other than baked beans. When I first arrived I refused to join them; I'd spent every night on the streets and I thought I was cool.'

'I bet they soon disabused you of that notion.' Fliss smiled softly.

Warmth and light flowed over him and Ash suddenly found himself laughing fondly.

'You got that right. Movie nights quickly became my favourite and Rosie and I used to love to sit together on the couch and eat popcorn. I even kept going around when I'd left foster care.'

'I remember you saying. I thought that was a lovely thing to do.'

'One night we were watching a film and just when some character was being buried the popcorn went off in the kitchen. Immediately she joked that when she was cremated, she wanted to have popcorn kernels in with her so that she could go out with a bang. For some reason we couldn't stop laughing and somehow it became a running joke, so when I saw that popcorn seller tonight it felt like it…meant something.'

'You're not really going to put the kernels in

the coffin?' Her face looked so concerned, so caring that he thought his heart was in a vice.

So much for keeping control of his emotions. For never letting anyone get too close to hurt him. He'd let Fliss in and when he hadn't been looking she'd begun to tear down his defences.

'Of course I'm not going to put them in the coffin.' He shook his head gently at her. 'But having them with me, it makes me feel like I haven't forgotten how close we were.'

'I get it, Ash. I do.'

Her quiet assurance somehow soothed his soul.

'But if you change your mind,' she offered. 'If you need anything. *Anything*, Ash.'

'I won't,' he told her quietly.

And then he took her again, both knowing it was for the last time. They stared at each other as he slid inside her. Until they were both driving it onwards, urgently, greedily, until she arched her whole body and called out as she tumbled into the abyss. And he cried her name and followed her.

Finally, he held her, dropping soft kisses on her body as her breathing eventually slowed and deepened and slumber overtook her. By the time he slipped silently from the bed, got dressed and left the room, Ash knew he had never found it harder to do the right thing.

* * *

The morning sun was streaming through the window by the time Fliss awoke again. Exquisitely sore, deliciously sated and inexplicably sad.

She rolled over, away from the empty space in the bed, and the dent on the pillow where Ash's head had rested only a few hours earlier. Picking up her phone, she checked the time.

Oh-eight-hundred hours. Ash's plane would be in the air and almost halfway home already.

The thought didn't help her churning stomach.

Last night had been everything she'd expected it would be and more. She'd been fooling herself if she thought she could manage a one-night stand with anyone, but certainly not with a man like Ash. He had made her feel alive in a way she'd never dreamed possible. Her entire body ached, from her breasts which he'd grazed with his stubble, to her neck which he'd grazed with his teeth, and between her legs which had experienced such delicious torture.

But the part which ached the most was deep inside her heart and she feared it would never heal. Her only consolation was that at least she'd got out now, before she'd fallen for Ash Stirling, head over heels.

Impulsively, she picked up her mobile and dialled the only person she could.

'Elle?' Sinking on the bed with relief at the sound of her friend's voice, she wondered how best to phrase her request, given that Elle only had two weeks of R&R with her fiancé before returning to Razorwire.

'I'm so sorry, but I could really use a chat right now...'

She tailed off, shutting down the part of her brain that was screaming, *I think I may have actually fallen for Ash.*

'Any chance I could call in to yours for an hour once I get back to the UK?'

'You could—' she heard Elle's hesitant voice crackle over the phone '—but I'm not there.'

A frown deepened on Fliss's face as she listened to her friend talk. Her explanation was so flimsy it could barely support its own weight. And the monotone voice was so different from Elle's habitually jovial tone as they agreed a time and place.

So just what the heck was Elle doing on her own in an airport hotel room about an hour out of the RAF base on the outskirts of Oxford, when she should have been a hundred miles away enjoying her last two days of R&R with her fiancé, Stevie?

* * *

Fliss eyed Elle curiously, wondering what had happened in the thirty hours since their phone call to bring about the change in her friend.

'Are you pregnant?' she accused. 'You're positively glowing, your eyes are all sparkly...'

'And my coat is shiny?' Elle cut across her, laughing. 'I'm sorry if I sounded...*off* during that conversation. You've no idea how relieved I was that you called; I really needed someone to talk to.'

'You and Stevie had a fight? Was it about the wedding plans again?'

She was trying to be sympathetic but all she really wanted to do was pour the whole story out to Elle.

'I walked in on him having sex in *our* bed, with some *groupie*.'

'Elle!' Her problems forgotten in an instant, Fliss was aghast.

"And that's not the first time."

Watching Elle's face colour with embarrassment, Fliss couldn't decide whether she was more upset for her friend, or angry on her behalf.

'How dare he do that to you.'

Elle must be devastated, Stevie was the only man she'd ever even kissed. Only the funny thing was, she didn't look devastated. To Fliss, her friend looked the way she herself had felt when she'd received the *Dear John* letter from Robert.

Relieved.

She couldn't help herself. Before she could stop it, she imagined what it would be like to have received a letter like that from Ash. Or to walk in on Ash that way.

It was like a physical body blow. Pain seared through her as Fliss grasped the edges of the chair, trying to steady herself and struggling to catch a breath.

That answered that question then, she realised in horror. So much for Ash being just a one-night fling.

'Are you okay?' She concentrated on her friend.

'Surprisingly, yes. I… I've been feeling Stevie and I were out of step for a while now.'

'I know.' Fliss was tentative. 'Maybe even years, looking back?'

'Maybe.'

They'd both been so indifferent about their respective fiancés, but Fliss had put it down to their careers.

'Now I understand why you sounded so deflated the other day on the phone. But now you look so buoyed?'

Fliss didn't add that it was the same way

she felt after her night with Ash. The idea of one-man Elle having a fling was disorientating. But maybe it would be the best thing her friend could do.

After all, hadn't her own fling with Ash stirred more emotions in her in four days than Robert ever had in four years? So where did that leave her?

'So much has happened since then,' Elle started, before stopping abruptly.

'Tell me about it!' Fliss attempted to roll her eyes light-heartedly; Elle would think she was crazy.

But for once Elle was too lost in her own thoughts to notice. Fliss could practically see the tussle on her friend's face as her friend debated whether or not to spill her story. Eventually, Elle shook her head in determination.

'No, *you* called *me*, Fliss. Which means this time *you* have to go first.'

'Since when do you and I stand on ceremony?'

She eyed her friend suspiciously and Elle offered a sheepish smile.

'Sorry, you're right. But I just need a bit more time to process. You go first.'

Fliss suppressed a groan, schooling herself to appear as normal as she could.

'I've no idea where to begin, either.'

'Okay.' Elle grinned suddenly. 'Remember what we did at uni? First animal to pop into your head. Don't think. Just say.'

'Dog.' Fliss floundered, thinking how unoriginal her answers had always been.

'Favourite colour?'

'Purple.'

'What's the big news?'

'I kissed Man Candy.'

A stunned silence filled the room, so loud Fliss could hear it thrumming in her ears. She willed Elle to say something. *Anything.*

'Are you serious?'

Fliss's heart flip-flopped. She hadn't realised how much she really wanted to hear Elle's approval.

'Serious.' She nodded. 'Well, more than just kissed, actually. We slept together. In a hotel. On the way home.'

It sounded so emotionless when she said the words, but nothing could be further from the truth.

'Are you shocked and appalled?'

'Shocked, yes. Appalled, no,' Elle marvelled. 'I know I suggested it, but I never really thought you'd go in for a fling. I'm so pleased; I think it's just what you needed after Robert.'

'You're right, of course,' Fliss began hesitantly. 'Only it wasn't just about having a fling;

it was about finding the person who made me want to have a fling.'

'Oh, no.' Elle peered at her. 'You've fallen for him, haven't you?'

Fliss attempted to look horrified. 'No. No, of course not. Well, not *fallen* for, exactly. Okay… maybe a bit.' She puffed up her cheeks and blew out. 'I need your help, Elle. What am I supposed to do now?'

'Don't ask me.' Elle shrugged, feigning nonchalance. 'Following our phone conversation I decided that I wasn't going to spend last night moping in my room, and so I went to some Latin-dance club. After fifteen years having only ever slept with one person, I have now slept with two.'

'You had a one-night stand?' Fliss gaped.

The coincidence of it was striking. Both she and Elle had always been so career-focused, so conservative in their personal lives, yet within twenty-four hours of meeting each other, they'd both had the first, and probably only, one-night stand of their lives.

'So you want to tell me how I'm supposed to do this, because I seem to have got the *fling-then-forget* bit a little messed up? What do we do now?' Fliss joked weakly.

'Don't ask me.' Elle shrugged. 'Only I think I may have fallen a little for my guy too. Not that he is even my guy. So I think that makes you and I a right pair of one-night-stand failures.'

She rolled her eyes and Fliss laughed.

'I think you're right. But hey, at least we can now say that we tried it.'

'Right. But now we just try to figure something out, and forget them.'

She looked about as dubious as Fliss felt and an image of Ash popped, unbidden, into her mind. The way he'd worked so in sync with her that first day. The way he'd come to that rooftop to tell her that Corporal Hollings was stable enough to be flown home. The way he'd listened to her at the table as she'd told him things she'd never told anyone before.

And then other images. The way he'd kissed her back at camp. The way he'd made her forget everything but him as he'd touched her so skilfully on that hillside over the carnival. The way he'd claimed her again and again, making her feel as though no man had ever understood her body, her needs, as he did.

White-hot flames licked at her insides, setting every inch of her skin on fire just at the memories. How was any man going to ever match up to Colonel Asher Stirling?

CHAPTER TEN

ASH STALLED AT the crematorium doors. For a moment he was seven again, and beyond the door wasn't his foster mum Rosie, but his mum.

Part of him wanted to turn and run but that wasn't in his nature. More concerning was the fact that another part of him wished that he hadn't been too proud to accept Fliss's offer to accompany him. If he had, she might be here now, standing right next to him.

But needing anyone wasn't in his nature either.

His nature was to push people away. To keep them at arm's length so they didn't see that weak part of him he'd never been able to fully eradicate. And in protecting himself he often ended up hurting others. Just as he had hurt Rosie. And Wilf. He hadn't intended to hurt them. And if he let Fliss in, he'd end up doing the same.

A hot pain stabbed through him at the idea of anyone ever hurting Fliss.

In one night she'd ignited such emotions in him. Passion, protectiveness, even possessiveness. He shook his head as if that would dislodge the memories of their night together. Memories which played on permanent loop in his brain.

Ironic, really.

He'd intended that night to be the distraction he needed from thinking about the funeral. Now he found he needed a distraction from thinking about that one night. Sex with Fliss was supposed to have been *just sex*. In the past it had always been *just sex*. Hot sex, wild sex, intense sex or lazy sex. It never mattered; the result had always been the same.

He'd tried to deny it but it had been different with Fliss, even from the start. And even when he'd walked out of the door, the memories had taken up residency in his head and refused to be evicted.

'Going inside, mate?'

The unfamiliar voice caught him unawares, snapping him out of his thoughts and reminding Ash why he was here.

The funeral.

He turned with something approaching relief. The expression on the stranger's face was instantly recognisable. A couple of years older than Ash but unmistakably another foster kid Rosie had helped. They nodded at each other in unspoken acknowledgement as Ash gestured for the other man to go ahead.

Stepping through the door, he stood just off to the side and straightened his service dress uniform and black arm band. The other man had made his way up the aisle to where Wilfred stood by the coffin.

Pain tightened Ash's chest.

His foster father looked old. So much older than Ash remembered. Where was the man mountain of Ash's childhood? It had only been, what? He calculated the last couple of tours. *Four years.* Four years since he'd last seen Wilf and Rosie—not that she'd recognised him—yet the frail old man in front of him could have been a decade and a half older. No doubt evidence of the toll Rosie's illness had taken on him.

Wilf greeted the other man with a hand-shake and a brief embrace, exchanging a few words before the man went to sit down. Emotions rushed Ash. He doubted his foster father would be as pleased to see *him.* He should have come back years ago. But he couldn't leave now, even if Wilf asked him to. He owed it to Rosie to be here.

Alone again, the old man resumed his stance, trying to straighten his back and steel himself against the emotions which were clearly flowing just beneath the surface. Typically stoic Wilfred.

He would stay strong for everyone else even though Ash imagined he was crumbling inside.

Then there were no more excuses. Ash forced himself to take his first step to the aisle, placing one foot in front of the other, until his foster father finally looked up and saw him.

'Asher.'

To Ash's shock the old man practically stumbled down the aisle towards him, gratitude and fondness in the watery eyes which were paler than he remembered. He hauled Ash into the tightest bear hug before suddenly appearing to lose all strength, the thin body slumping against his own as Wilf clung on in silence, only his frail, shaking body, betraying himself to his former foster son. And then Ash finally allowed himself to feel. He wrapped his arms around the man who had helped to save his life and they hugged each other for several long moments.

By the time Wilf patted his arms, standing up again and looking him in the eye, the old man's face was slightly wet.

'Thank you. She'd be so happy you came.' He exhaled deeply. '*I'm* so happy you came. And in your uniform. Rosie always loved to see you dressed like that. She was so proud of you. We both were.'

He stopped, choked up, filled with the love

Ash recalled so well. Remorse flooded his entire body.

He'd been such a fool and now it was too late.

'I'm sorry.' He shook his head. 'I'm so sorry.'

'You have nothing to be sorry for, son. Nothing. You hear me?'

Something clogged in Ash's throat and he swallowed painfully. 'I should have come a long time ago.'

Bony fingers clutched his arm.

'You were fighting for your country. Hell, you nearly made the ultimate sacrifice when that grenade went off.' He led Ash up to the coffin, resuming his former position next to it, but this time facing Ash. 'And you never dealt with losing your own mum. I understand why you couldn't deal with losing Rosie too.'

'I should never have left it so damn long,' Ash bit out, his voice cracking.

'Rosie didn't know any different. Not by then. She didn't even know me. She wouldn't have known you and you'd have put yourself through hell for no good reason.'

'I let you down.' The words came out by themselves.

Wilf cast him a ferocious stare. 'You most certainly did not. You were there when she needed you. You made her prouder than you know, as an army officer but, more importantly, as an honourable man. You have no idea how proud I was when I heard you'd become a colonel.'

Even after everything, Wilf had been following his career?

Guilt flooded through Ash, making him feel sick.

'I should sit down,' he managed thickly. 'People will want to…speak to you.'

He couldn't say the words.

'Stand with me?' the old man asked suddenly. 'Please?'

It felt like an honour he didn't deserve.

'I…shouldn't.'

A hopeful light danced momentarily in Wilf's eyes as he peered around the building.

'You came with someone?'

'No.' Ash hated snuffing out that light.

'Still haven't met *the one*? You will.' Wilf nodded firmly. 'Rosie always said that one day you'd meet the woman who would complete you and you'd stop fighting the idea of opening your life to someone.'

It took everything Ash had to shut out images of the other night. He'd spent thirty hours trying to convince himself it was *just sex,* but deep down he knew he was going to have to face up to the connection they'd forged when he hadn't been looking. Maybe it had been when they'd worked together so fluidly out in the field, or maybe on that rooftop when he'd told her about the scars, or maybe when she'd opened up to him at the carnival about her past.

At some point he was going to have to admit that it wasn't *just sex* at all.

And once he accepted it, perhaps he could finally put it behind him.

'That's not for me. My career…isn't conducive to a relationship.'

Wilf snorted. 'When you meet your one, everything else will fall into place.'

Before he could answer, more people arrived and made their way to Wilf to express their condolences, and Ash was left alone with his thoughts.

It was no use. He was helpless against the memories of Fliss which assaulted him on multiple levels. From the sweet sound of her laughter and the silky-soft cascade of that blonde hair, to the intoxicating scent of her hot core and the honey taste of her climax on his tongue.

And now he craved more.

But neither he nor Fliss could afford more. They were both dedicated to their Army careers, and the reason they were both so successful was because they didn't have distractions. He knew so many soldiers who left their 'family head' at RAF Lyneham and put on their

'Army head' when they went on operations. But, even then, the smallest thing could throw them, whether news from home or just missing a loved one that day.

Avoiding being tied down meant he never had to worry about that, and Fliss was the same. Which was why they could each focus on their respective tasks and know they would always give everything they had.

He needed to forget Fliss. Get back to life as he'd known it a month ago.

'You're a good boy,' Wilf said softly as they were left alone again. 'You deserve love. But, like my Rosie always said, you just need to let go. You're the only one standing in the way of your own happiness.'

Ash stood firm. 'I'm happy,' he lied. 'Anyway, what can I do for you, Wilf?'

'You're here. That's all I need.'

'Okay.'

Standing together in companionable silence, Ash forced a polite smile to his lips as each new arrival came up to Wilf. Rosie had a good send-off. He wasn't surprised. She'd been an incredible woman.

It felt like an eternity before the two men had to take their own seats. But, just as they were about to move, Wilf placed a hand on Ash's arm, his grip surprisingly strong and his eyes suddenly sharp.

'Did you bring anything with you?' he demanded urgently.

Sheepishly, as if he were fourteen again, Ash reached into his pocket and took out a handful of popcorn kernels.

The grin split Wilf's face in two even as a tear tipped over and rolled down his cheek.

'Me too. I already threw mine in,' he chuckled. 'We'll send our Rosie off with the bang she always wanted.'

'Ash?'

When Fliss opened her front door at such an ungodly hour, he was the last person she expected to see.

Ever since she'd awoken in that hotel room alone, she hadn't been able to shake the hope that she might see him again. It wasn't just about the sex, but if that was all he was offering then, so help her, she'd take it.

He was exhausted and devastated, and looking dishevelled in his service dress. Her heart vaulted around her chest, questions piling in on her. But, before she could ask a single one, he stepped through the door, tugged apart the tie of her dressing gown and scooped her up, encouraging her to wrap her legs around his hips as he pinned her against the hallway wall. Fliss was vaguely aware of the front door slamming behind him.

'Bedroom?' he ground out hoarsely, abandoning her mouth for a brief moment.

She was barely able to think straight, let alone speak.

'Left, right, right,' she managed.

It never crossed her mind to stop him. But she wanted him too much. Wanted *this* too much. They'd have to deal with the fallout later.

He laid her on the bed, stripping her down so that she felt the cool morning air on her body, sending goosebumps skittering over her skin and hardening her nipples. Ash noticed too, studying her whole body reverently before covering each breast with a large hand and taking both brown peaks between a finger and his thumbs so that sparks shot through her body.

But he wasn't here at this hour for foreplay. Moments later, they were both naked and he was covering her pliant body with his own solid one, holding himself above her, his eyes locked with hers, not a word more spoken. Neither of them needed words. And then Ash claimed her as his, quickly bringing her to orgasm moments before he exploded inside her.

It was only when their shudders had subsided that he slipped out of her, still caressing her spine as he would a lover, until finally his breathing slowed and he drifted into the first sleep Fliss suspected he'd had since leaving the hotel the other day.

When she woke several hours later the bed was cold, like some pathetic déjà-vu. Only this time, she realised, something felt different. Throwing on an old T-shirt and yoga pants, she padded along the corridor, following the scent of coffee and warm bread. He was dressed in gym gear that she imagined he'd retrieved from a gym bag he kept in the boot of his car, just as she did.

Then her eyes widened in surprise. 'Home-made bread?'

'Rosie taught me,' he answered simply.

She took it for the hedged invitation that it was. Moving gingerly into the room, she slid onto a barstool across the kitchen worktop, as though any sudden moves might startle him.

He watched her, his gaze unwavering. 'I'm sorry about this morning. That wasn't what I intended when I drove here.'

'It wasn't?' She attempted to tease him in an effort to conceal her nerves, but she knew it sounded a little stiff, a little awkward.

The truth was that she didn't want to hear the words. She didn't want him to say it had been a mistake.

Instead, he offered a wry smile. 'Okay, it was. But not like that. I wanted to talk first.'

Something pulled in her chest but she schooled her features, scared to give too much away.

'Oh?'

He raked his hand through his hair, clearly trying to work out where to start. Her heart paused for a beat. The apprehensive gesture was so unlike the man she had come to know.

'I'm sorry.' He blew out a sharp breath. 'I seem to be saying that word a lot recently. But I don't know where to start.'

She had to be careful here. 'How did the funeral go?'

Another pause.

'It was harrowing,' he confessed at last, then frowned. 'Yet somehow…soothing.'

'You got some closure,' she observed.

He rolled his eyes. 'Is that the quack term for it?'

Ah, that flash of macho pride she recognised from too many soldiers, the stigma that still, to some degree, shrouded talking about personal issues.

'Don't knock it,' she warned patiently. 'Or underestimate its significance.'

'Fine. Then I guess I got *closure*.' He bunched his shoulders. 'And I *am* sorry. I was out of line when I told you to mind your own business in the hotel that night. You were right; I wasn't mentally prepared for the funeral. I *did* need to say goodbye and I *did* need permission to feel those emotions. I'm grateful to you for saying all you did; it made me open my mind up subconsciously so it wasn't such a shock when I got there.'

'And your foster father?'

'Yeah,' he admitted. 'You were right too. Wilf welcomed me straight away. Hugged me. Told me he was glad I was there.'

'Good,' she offered softly, relieved she had judged it right.

Nonetheless, it was clear from Ash's changing expression that there was more to it than he was saying. She could practically hear the cogs clicking over in his head, and as he brooded she could feel something building. At first, she couldn't put a name to it. She just needed to give him space to find the right words for whatever it was he wanted to tell her.

'I felt I'd let him down. And Rosie.'

He raked his hand through his hair, short as it was. The helplessness of the gesture tugged at her.

'You're not the kind of person to let people down,' she protested. 'I spoke to your men. Remember?'

His jaw locked, the tiny pulse flickering. Finally, she could pinpoint the source of the tension building inside him. *Guilt and anger.*

'It's not the same,' he growled.

'Why not?' she ventured.

He crossed his arms defensively over his chest, subconsciously pushing her away. She could tell he wished the conversation was over but he felt obliged to answer. She was putting herself in his sights. She didn't know why she was even doing it. She didn't have to. They weren't even a couple.

He turned his back, busying himself with emptying the now cold cafetière and boiling the kettle for a fresh one. She knew he was buying time. Silently she watched, waiting for him to continue.

All at once, a realisation detonated in her brain.

You're going to get hurt because you've let yourself care about him, you stupid girl.

Before she had a chance to regroup, Ash started speaking and inexorably she was drawn back in.

'I told you how Wilf and Rosie turned my life around? Pretty much saved me?'

'You told me they did, yes. Though not how.'

'Well, when I got busted for stealing the car, no one else was prepared to take me on. Except for them. They were tough, but fair. They told me that they were my last chance saloon. That they could see I had the potential for more but they weren't prepared to take chance after chance on me. That this was my opportunity to lose.'

'They were tough but fair,' she acknowledged.

'Right. They told me what they were prepared to do for me, and also what they expected from me in return. Not least that every hour of my day was going to be accounted for so that I had no time to pick back up with my so-called mates.'

'Was that hard?' she asked curiously.

Even now, the relief in his expression was evident.

'No. It was the excuse I needed to change my life. I knew those guys were no good for me but they were all I had. I never believed Rosie and Wilf would be there for me when it really came down to it, but I was prepared to use them to get out of the cruddy life I had.'

'But they *were* there for you, right?'

'Yes. They were. It took time, but I finally began to see that the more I gave, the more they gave. Rosie tutored me to get my grades back up—no one had ever given a damn about my grades before. Then, when I succeeded there, Wilf found me a job in his garage as a mechanic to earn a bit of money. *My* money, which I could spend however I wanted to.'

'Unlike the foster father who beat you when you were late from a paper round because he'd been waiting for his drinking money,' Fliss recalled.

The memory of him telling her that still punched a hole in her stomach.

'Right. And I responded to the discipline. I respected them for being honourable and fair. Within the year they'd turned me around and got me into the Army Cadet Force. I never looked back.'

He was making it sound easier than it clearly had been. She could only imagine the effort Ash must have made too, to turn his life around.

'I managed to get sponsorship for my engineering degree, an Army Undergraduate Bursary, but I still couldn't afford to go. And then Rosie and Wilf came forward with the money.'

Fliss gasped. 'They can't have afforded to do that for all their foster kids.'

'They couldn't. I hadn't even lived with them for a couple of years, but we'd stayed in contact. They'd made sure of it. Everything I've achieved—my career, being a colonel—is all down to the opportunity they gave me. I could never have dreamed of this life if not for Rosie and Wilf.'

His humility was striking. She wanted to point out that they never would have offered him that support if he hadn't been worthy of it. If he hadn't been Ash. But he wouldn't thank her for it; he was still battling demons for some perceived failing and this was a rare glimpse at the vulnerable side of Colonel Asher Stirling. A side no one else ever got to see. As sad as she was for Ash, she couldn't help feel special that he trusted her in this way.

Fliss bit her tongue.

'Rosie and Wilf were my guests when I had my passing out parade at Sandhurst. They were the family I brought to any officer bails, or garden parties. They were the people I called first every time I got a promotion. I visited them once or twice a year. More, if I wasn't on a tour of duty.'

'You stayed close,' Fliss said softly. 'There's nothing wrong in that.'

In fact it made her wonder, when he had such a support network like them, why he'd become so closed off. So afraid to let other people in.

'And then Rosie started showing the first signs of Alzheimer's. Small things at first, forgetting people's names, telling the same story a few times over the course of a weekend, and it was gradual. But, because I was away so much, every time I went back there was something new.'

Silently, Fliss listened to him.

'She started forgetting medication, eating through a whole box of twenty ice-creams in an hour because she couldn't remember having had one, running out into the street screaming with fear because Wilf had left her alone for five minutes to go and buy a pint of milk. By the time a few years had gone by it had got to the point where she couldn't recognise anyone. Sometimes not even Wilf.'

'That must have been hard.'

The silence hung between them. She held her breath, the urge to touch him, comfort him almost overwhelming, but she didn't dare to. They were getting to the root of the issue but if she said anything, if she pushed him, he could shut her out entirely. She sat immobile, hardly even breathing, willing him to trust her enough to continue.

'Frankly, I didn't handle it well,' Ash stated simply.

For a man who liked to stay in control as much as Ash did, she could only imagine how painful that was for him to admit.

'I returned from a tour four years ago and she didn't know who I was at all. When I tried to tell her, she became hysterical, screaming that I was lying and that the real Ash was only a kid. She warned me not to go anywhere near Ash because he was doing well and she didn't want me pulling him back down the wrong path.'

'She thought she was looking out for the fourteen-year-old Ash again,' Fliss realised.

'Right. And she had no idea that *I* was Ash.' His expression was flat but there was no missing the pain behind those shale-hued eyes. 'I was away so much with the Army and my sporadic presence was only stressing her out, so Wilf and I agreed that it would be better if I didn't see her.'

It must have been like losing his mother all over again, Fliss realised abruptly. Feeling rejected all over again, feeling as if it was him against everyone all over again.

Of all people, she should know how deep that rejection cut. It would be like losing her uncle, the only person who had believed in her.

'But how did you handle it badly? You did nothing wrong,' Fliss pointed out carefully. 'You stayed away because it was the kindest thing to do.'

'I left Wilf to cope all alone. I might not have been able to see Rosie, but I could have pretended to be someone else. I could have been there for Wilf instead of just dumping him in it.'

'Ash, you were off fighting for your country.

You're a colonel. You were a major then. The career path we've chosen isn't like other jobs. There are sacrifices. Wilf and Rosie understood, even before the Alzheimer's. With the best will in the world, you couldn't have been there.'

'I should have found a way. I should have taken fewer postings away, fewer tours of duty.'

'But no way would you have ever made colonel. At your level that would have been your career over.'

'I should have made that sacrifice for Rosie. And for Wilf.'

It was the grief talking, she knew that. His mind grappling with an impossible situation. In time he would see that, but for now all she could do was tell him what she thought he needed to hear.

'I don't believe she would ever have wanted you to do that. From what you've told me about them, I don't think either of them would have thanked you for it. They didn't make those sacrifices to send you to Cadets, to fund you through university for you to walk away from it. You could never have gone back.'

'I should have done it anyway. I could have found a job in Civvy Street, moved in next door. Even if I couldn't have been there to help care for Rosie, I could have been there for Wilf whilst *he* cared for her.'

'That's a hell of a thing to ask of anyone.' Fliss shook her head. 'I know you like to think of yourself as superhuman, Ash, and I know your men see you as their hero, but guess what? You *are* only human. You have emotions and you were in pain. I don't believe Wilf thinks you abandoned him.'

'It's not about what Wilf thinks. He can tell me there was no other choice all he likes,' he bit out angrily. But she knew it was anger directed at himself, not at her. 'It's about what *I* know. And I know I could have done more. *Should* have done more. I should have found a way.'

A tight hand was squeezing Fliss's heart inside her chest. His pain was palpable. He'd lost one of the only two people who had cared for him, loved him. And he was alienating himself from the other person because he couldn't shake a sense of guilt which he shouldn't be feeling.

No wonder he kept with short-term relationships, never opening himself up to more hurt. Just like her. They were two of a kind.

So maybe they could help each other? The thought stole into Fliss's brain so softly that she didn't realise it was there at first. She brushed it away and calmed her fluttering heart.

It was a ridiculous idea.

'Thanks,' he said suddenly. 'For listening.

This wasn't what you bargained for when we agreed to this one-off fling.'

She managed a nervous laugh. 'It's not a problem. Besides, I told you I didn't usually do one-night stands. Now I can say I definitely have had one. And I'm glad—one night wasn't enough.'

She just about succeeded in not clapping her hand over her mouth at her *faux-pas*, but, rather than distrust, the look Ash shot her was so brooding, so licentious, her body shivered under its intensity.

'One night was most definitely *not* enough.'

She couldn't speak; she could only jerk her head.

He stood up abruptly, pacing her tiny kitchen as though deciding whether or not to say anything more.

'We have two weeks' R&R, Fliss. Aside from a one-day course, which is in this neck of the woods anyway, and a rugby match with my former battalion, I'm not expected anywhere.'

'Okay.'

'What about you?'

'Nowhere,' she confirmed, feeling as though she was trapped in some kind of suspension.

She was almost afraid to think he was suggesting what she wanted with every fibre of her being. Afraid to say it and be wrong and experience rejection on a level she had never known possible.

'What are you saying, Ash?' she breathed.

'I'm saying, to hell with it. We have two weeks and no one else with demands on our time. Let's spend it together.'

Fliss felt as though she were burning up inside, consumed by the need to say *yes,* but her brain told her *no.* If she'd fallen for him this hard after one night, then how far gone would she be after another fourteen nights? And what about the feeling of rejection, of loss at the end of it? Logically, she knew Ash couldn't reject her if they had agreed the terms to start with. But man, she was going to have to keep reminding herself of that.

'Two weeks?' she whispered.

'Two weeks,' he confirmed.

Two weeks to slake this all-consuming hunger they had for each other? She doubted two lifetimes would even be enough. But deep down she knew she'd take two minutes if that was all that was on offer.

'Fine.' She nodded as he strode over to capture her face in his hands and drop a kiss onto her lips. 'Two weeks it is.'

CHAPTER ELEVEN

'OKAY, SO FORGET the golden hour, gentlemen, this is the platinum ten minutes.' Fliss cast her eyes around the bunch of primarily green-gilled young soldiers in front of her and wondered how many of them would be out on the front line within months.

This was a taster day before the main pre-mob training which would take place down the line but, to Fliss, every opportunity to teach these guys how to help save lives gave her a greater window when she was back with her MERT.

'With battlefield injuries, statistics have shown that the majority of fatalities occur within the first ten minutes of the wounding, so every second counts. The MERT can't get to you in that time, however fast you call it in. So it's down to you and the unit medics on the ground at the time.'

Her skin prickled, telling her that Ash had entered the outdoor teaching area behind her. In the last ten days together she seemed to have developed a heightened awareness of his presence, and she was dreading what it would be like when the two weeks finally drew to an end. Far from slaking their desire, each passing day had only seemed to stoke it even higher.

She had no idea where they stood.

They'd never discussed a time frame after that first day, but the fact that Ash had found her a last-minute teaching spot on the course he was running—just so that they didn't have to spend one of their precious days apart—only made her all the more confused.

All she could do was ride it out, enjoy it and accept the inevitable. And doing the best damned job she could on the course today should help to remind her of the career she loved, and ease her into life post-Ash as seamlessly as possible.

'We've been seeing remarkable numbers of soldiers surviving when they might previously have died from their injuries and that's in no small part down to you guys. Where there are penetrating wounds, whether from rounds, knives, shrapnel or injuries requiring multiple amputation, blood loss at the scene can mean the casualty is dead before we can get in that heli and get to you. So one of your priorities is learning to staunch severe bleeding and applying tourniquets correctly.'

She thought of Ash and the extent of his grenade scar, something unidentifiable tearing through her. If he hadn't had good buddies fighting to save him before that MERT had arrived, she wouldn't have even known he existed.

She would never have had these last two weeks. Never have known what *alive* could feel like.

The truth hit her hard.

She was going to tell him how she felt.

Tonight. She would lay it all out there. And if he rejected her, then so what? She stomped down the ugly fear which threatened to weaken her resolve. At least she would know. It couldn't be any worse than wondering what might have happened if she'd only had the courage to try.

'Right, so *you*, come over here and be my casualty and *you*, bring your kit up; you're about to learn how to save your buddy's life.'

Ash barely noticed the return drive home, slipping easily through the gears as they sped down the quiet streets, the late night traffic at a minimum.

Even the lights seemed to be in his favour, turning green as he approached as though cheering him on.

He had to tell her.

In three days, their time together would be

over. At least, their self-imposed two-week time limit would be up. But Ash already knew he didn't want to give Fliss up, *couldn't* give her up. She felt the same way, he knew it. From the way she looked at him, talked with him, making the most mundane things sound compelling when they were uttered by her lips, to the way she clung to him, crying out his name as she gave herself up to him so completely when they made love.

He had no idea how or when she'd peeled away every last piece of his defences, he just knew that it had started from the minute she'd walked into that tent at Razorwire, all lithe body, long legs and flashing eyes. And it hadn't stopped since.

The time limit had only served to highlight to Ash how precious time was. He needed Fliss in his arms, his bed, his life, for as long as they both drew breath.

And tonight he realised he had to tell her that. He didn't want to wait any longer for them to begin building a different future. Together.

'Whose car is that?' He glowered as they finally rounded the corner to her street and he saw the unfamiliar vehicle in the drive.

His first guess would have been her uncle, but it was far too beaten-up and pranged to be the General's car.

'Stop here!' Her abrupt cry caught him off-guard.

Assuming she'd seen a cat or a fox, he executed an emergency stop in the dark street, glancing around for the culprit, but nothing moved except for a breeze through the trees.

'Wait, what are you doing?'

Beside him, Fliss was scrabbling to release her seat belt. Ash caught her hand to still her, but she wrenched it free with a force he didn't recognise. He said her name, then shouted it but she didn't even seem aware he was still there.

'Fliss? Fliss! Look at me.'

Taking her chin firmly in his hand, it took Ash two attempts to persuade her to look at him. When she did, she finally seemed to take a breath, although the fearful expression didn't diminish.

'Relax. Breathe. What's going on?'

'It's my mother,' she mumbled eventually.

Her eyes, so uncharacteristically dull, fearful and something else he couldn't quite read, knocked the breath from him. A blast even more lethal than the grenade which had almost taken his life. It commanded every defensive, protective emotion in him.

'In your house?'

'She's my mother. She pops round from time to time.'

'Define *time to time.*'

She glared at him. He didn't know whether to celebrate the fact that the dullness had disappeared, or object to the fact that any rage appeared to be directed at him.

'Once or twice a year.'

'And she has a key?'

'She's my mother.'

'A title, by all accounts, which she doesn't deserve.' He slammed his palm on the steering wheel, desperate to make her see sense. 'For pity's sake, Fliss, you're better than this. You *deserve* better than this.'

'Any relationship with her is better than nothing.' Her defensive tone had the same unidentifiable edge to it that her eyes had and Ash couldn't shake the feeling he was missing something, but he had no idea what. He filed it away for later.

'No, it isn't. Not when it causes you to react like *this* at the sight of her car.' He raked his hand through his hair, his feelings for Fliss all jumbling around in his chest. 'How do I make you see this isn't normal, it isn't right? I thought you said she used to rage at you, anyway?'

'Sometimes.' He could tell she wished she'd never told him anything at all. 'But sometimes things are…nice.'

'Why?' He was instantly suspicious. 'Does she want something?'

Glowering at him, Fliss refused to answer.

The answer was obvious to him. *Money.* Inevitably, it would be about money. He wanted to say more, wanted to make Fliss see. But he could feel her slipping away from him already. They hadn't had long enough together for her to trust him. As far as she was concerned, in a few days he would be gone, and her uncle, and sporadic visits from her needy mother, would be all she had.

He should have told her he was falling in love with her before. And he should never have put some stupid time limit on their relationship. Now, all that would have to wait. For now he would have to change tack and wait it out.

'She can't hurt you,' he told her. 'Not unless *you* let her. I'll be here to support you.'

'No!' The cry almost shook the car. 'No, you can't come in.'

Ash gritted his teeth. 'Try to stop me.'

'I don't know what mood she'll be in, but either way she won't like it. It will just make things worse.'

Ash heard her desperation, and realised he'd do anything to erase it. Anything to hear her jaunty, sing-song voice right now.

'We won't let her.'

'*We?*'

'It's going to be okay,' he soothed, re-buckling her seat belt and turning in his seat to drive the car down the road and into a parking space outside the house. It didn't escape his notice that Fliss's mother had taken the single driveway space she must have known her daughter would use.

'Take as long as you need,' Ash said quietly as he turned the engine off and made no move to rush Fliss. 'We'll only go in when you're ready.'

This wasn't how she wanted to spend tonight, Fliss realised as she finally swung herself out of the car and forced leaden legs to carry her to the front door.

Her whole life, she'd dropped everything any time her mother had deigned to visit. Tonight was the first time she'd resented the intrusion.

Because there, beneath the flurry of fear and niggle of resentment, sat the ever-present embers of hope. Maybe, just maybe, this time would be different. Especially with Ash by her side.

Warily, Fliss slotted her key in the lock and turned it, a heaviness pressing in on her as she stepped through the door.

'Darling, you're back. I was afraid I might have missed you.'

So it was money she needed. Still, the embers of hope flickered. It meant it was going to be one of her more pleasant visits, as long as Fliss read her mum's signals and found the perfect opportunity to offer the funds without it looking like charity.

Not for the first time, Fliss felt a niggle of uncertainty.

It might be *darling* now, but on another occasion it could be any number of unrepeatable words.

What was she doing?

She hadn't needed Ash to tell her it was a toxic relationship, but she'd always clung on to it anyway. She'd never had the courage in the past to consider walking away. But with Ash here beside her...who knew?

'Mum.'

Fliss allowed herself to be swept up in the wide embrace, then stepped aside as her mother spotted Ash. An undisguised look of shock clouded her face before she greeted him with a decidedly coquettish air, and Fliss didn't miss the way he held her slightly away from his body as he shot Fliss a pointed look.

The fact that he held his opinions in check for her sake bolstered her confidence all the more.

'So this is your famous surgeon fiancé, darling? No wonder she's kept you hidden from me all these years, Robert dear. I have to say you're not what I expected. I didn't think you had it in you, Flissy.'

The needling comment found its mark perfectly as Fliss covered her chest as though to protect herself. The meaning, to Fliss, was clear—what was he doing with her? She only hoped Ash couldn't read it as clearly. Obviously her mother was piqued at the thought her daughter had done so well in her choice of partner.

'Ash Stirling,' Ash corrected her politely.

'Robert and I broke up.' Fliss didn't know why she avoided eye contact with Ash. She had no reason to feel guilt, but it suffused her body anyway. As though her mother's comments negated the fact that Fliss had told Ash that there had been someone before they'd met.

'Oh, I'm so sorry to hear that, but I suppose it was inevitable when you consider how successful a surgeon he was.' She swung back to Ash with a beam. 'And of course I can see you're a colonel. So you work together?'

'Ash is infantry, Mum. We were just running a course together today and Ash ran me home.'

'How thrillingly clandestine for you, Flissy darling.'

As if aware of what she was doing, Ash

stepped forward and placed his arm very point-edly around her shoulder. In that moment, she would have given anything to turn in to him and have him hold her. Hold her until her mother finally went away.

Years of barbed comments, nasty digs and cruel undermining—and her mother hadn't even got started so far tonight. And for what?

'Actually, *Fliss* and I were about to go out for a romantic meal,' Ash emphasised. 'But, of course, if you'd like to join us…?'

'Sounds fabulous. I'll grab my purse.' As she passed Fliss she poked a finger into her chest which was just a little too aggressive for fun. 'You do love to punch above your weight, don't you, darling? I've got to give you that much.'

Rage burned through Ash, as it had done for the last few hours since they'd walked into Fliss's home and met her mother.

Rage and an interminable disquiet that, over the course of the evening, the snipes and derisory comments had destroyed the Fliss he knew. The Fliss he had begun to fall in love with. Right now, his fiery, loving, spirited Fliss was barely a shell of herself. Ash could easily see how her mother, in one of her less amiable moods, would have raged at her daughter, whether Fliss was four or forty.

It had taken every last ounce of his self-control not to retaliate on Fliss's behalf. But now they were back at the house and finally alone in the kitchen, he found that he couldn't smother his ire any longer.

'You can't keep doing this, Fliss.' He swung her round, taking the cafetière from her shaking fingers and placing his hands on her shoulders. 'You need to say something.'

Misery emanated from her as she dropped her head to her chest in defeat, but still she managed to shake it weakly from one side to the other.

'You have to,' he growled. 'If you don't, I will.'

'You can't,' she gasped, her head jerking up painfully fast.

'Someone has to.'

'But not you,' she whispered fiercely, shaking his hands away.

The fight was there. He could see it; he just didn't know how to bring it out of her.

'Can't you see what she does to you?' His voice softened. 'Even now? The Fliss I know—the courageous, loyal, passionate woman, the skilled, dedicated, driven trauma doctor—has gone and this…this sullen, irascible teenager is in her place. It isn't healthy.'

'I know that.' He had to strain to hear the

words she mumbled so quietly. 'But I can't. I can't do it.'

'Yes, you can. I know you can.'

'I keep hoping.'

'For a different outcome?' He barely managed to disguise the contempt in his voice. 'Don't bother. She'll never change, I know the type.'

'She might.'

'She won't.' He put his hands back on her shoulders. 'You need to do this. And I need you to do this.'

The tiny light which usually sparked so brightly in her eyes flickered faintly back into life; its significance left Ash winded.

'Why?'

'Because I love you.'

He'd thought saying the words would be difficult. He was wrong.

'I love you,' he repeated, the words practically singing in his ears. They sounded good. They sounded natural. They sounded *right*.

She stared at him incredulously and then shook her head.

'No, you don't. You can't.'

'I love you,' he said firmly. 'But you're right. I love the bright, animated, confident Major Felicity Delaunay, who leaps off helis and stands up to arrogant colonels who she's only just met. I don't love this husk-like version of you.'

'We're the same person, Ash.'

'No, you aren't. And I can't be around that version. Tonight, your mother has stripped out every last bit of character and confidence and essence of *Fliss,* and you let her. I can't watch you let someone do that to you, year in and year out.'

His voice was thick with emotion; he hadn't felt so utterly trapped and powerless in a long time. He'd sworn as a kid he'd never go through that again and he knew, for his own sanity, that he couldn't afford to break that oath.

He could only hope to make Fliss understand, because she was the one who held the power to save them both.

'I've spent the entire evening barely able to keep a grip on my self-control. That isn't something I can keep doing, Fliss. It's destructive and I won't let myself go down that road. You *have* to put an end to this madness.'

'You're asking me to choose between you and my mother?'

The look she cast him was one of pure anguish that sought to rend his very soul.

'No. I'm asking you to choose between *you* and your mother. You need to cut all ties with her because, until you do, nothing is ever going to change and you're worth more than…*this*. A poor carbon copy of the Fliss I know.'

The slow, mocking clap behind him made them both start.

'Well, that was very touching, *darling*. But you can't honestly expect my daughter to choose a temporary fling like you over her own mother?'

'Fliss,' he said quietly.

Ash willed her to speak out with every fibre of his being. He could do it for her, he had no issue with that, but ultimately it wouldn't mean anything. This was something Fliss had to do for herself.

'You can do this.'

She didn't speak, didn't move.

'I rather think you have your answer.'

The triumphant tone was unmistakable but Ash didn't care. His only concern was the woman he now knew for certain that he loved. The question was whether she loved him enough to come back to him now.

The silence seemed to smother him.

He *did* have her answer.

But it wasn't an answer he could live with. For his own sake, he had to walk away.

Wordlessly, Ash strode into the bedroom, shoved his belongings into his overnight bag, all the while straining to hear Fliss. His gear packed, he slung the bag over his shoulder and headed back out into the hallway. Fliss hadn't even moved from her spot in the kitchen.

Something inside finally shattered into a million pieces as Ash left without a backward glance.

He couldn't afford one.

CHAPTER TWELVE

'I WOULDN'T WORRY about it, darling; it's for the best. You were never going to be able to hold onto a man like that, anyway.'

Fliss turned, the exultation in her mother's expression like a slap on the face. But she was already reeling from everything Ash had said.

He loved her?

He loved her?

It had sounded too incredible to be true. The ground had pitched and shifted beneath her feet and all she'd been able to focus on had been staying upright as she'd tried to work out how her entire world had now changed.

He'd told her she was *worth more*. Told her that she *deserved more*. And she'd thought talk was cheap, but he'd proved it to her by telling her he loved her. It had been like watching a fireworks display—the Army kind her uncle had taken her to where they'd used up all the end-of-year pyrotechnics for a display that surpassed anything in the civilian world. Just like being with Ash surpassed any other relationship she'd ever known in her life.

She understood why he'd said he couldn't be around her if she couldn't even stand up for herself. She'd known all evening that his iron control was slipping but she hadn't been able to help him, because that would have meant helping herself. And she hadn't thought she was good enough for that.

Ash had proved to her she was, and she'd been so stunned that she hadn't reacted fast enough.

And now she'd lost him.

But he'd still left her with a choice of her own. To accept her life as it was, her relationships as they were, or to finally stand up for herself. The least she could do was ensure that losing him wasn't for nothing.

She turned to her mother, determined to find out whether the chasm between them had ever stood a chance of being bridged or whether Ash was right, and her mother would never change.

'Do you really hate me that much?'

She could feel the chill hit the room.

'Don't start believing your little lover's words now,' her mother warned, her voice so sharp that it could have cut through Fliss deeper than any physical wound.

And it would have. Before Ash.

'*Do* you hate me?' She advanced on her mother, a tiny sliver of her old self returning with each step.

In an instant, her mother's face twisted into a smile that was too ugly to be anything but loathing.

'You ruined my only chance at happiness the day you were born.'

'You knew your dancing was over when you realised you were pregnant.' Fliss wasn't trying to antagonise, but it was something she'd always wondered about and never understood.

'Why didn't you get rid of me if you felt that strongly? Why have a child only to put it through such utter hell?'

'You think that isn't what I tried to do?' her mother spat, the truth embedding itself into Fliss's very being.

'Why did you change your mind?' she whispered.

There was no regret, no empathy, no love in her mother's reply. The scornful tone like applying heat to a burn.

'I didn't change my mind. I was more than happy to go through with it. But then your grandfather turned up, stormed in and frogmarched me out. White gown and all. There was no way he and your grandmother were ever going to allow me to do something that would shame them even more than they already were by my pregnancy.'

Rushing blood roared in her ears as she clawed at the edge of nothingness with her fingernails, just to try to find a purchase.

'I'd made a mistake, yes, I'd got pregnant. But the obvious solution to get rid of it wasn't even a consideration for them. That would be letting me off too lightly; in their eyes I was going to have to live with the consequences.'

'So because they'd trapped you into a miserable life, you made mine even worse?' Fliss cried.

'I tried to get out of there, I took you with me so that you wouldn't be brought up with the same restrictions I'd had. But the first chance you got, you went running back to them. You chose them over me,' her mother raged, her face inches away from Fliss's.

'I was eight!'

'You threw everything I did for you back in my face.'

'You did *nothing* for me,' Fliss argued, standing up to her mother for the first time in her life. 'Except make my life more wretched than it needed to be.'

It was almost too much to take in. Feeling for a chair, Fliss backed up and sat down. Ash had been right. Nothing she could say or do would make a difference to her mother. She was craving affection which was never going to come.

Repeating the cycle would only hurt more people. She'd been hurting herself, and she'd definitely been hurting Ash. They deserved better than that.

Maybe it wasn't too late.

Standing up on shaky legs, Fliss fixed her mother with a calm, firm stare. Her major's stare.

'I think it's time you left.'

Her mother snorted, deliberately turning her back.

Fliss inched her way to the door, fumbling with the catch as she hauled it open. It felt heavy, almost too heavy, but she gritted her teeth. 'I said, it's time you left.'

Her mother gave a bark of laughter. 'I don't think so, Felicity.' She didn't sound as sure of herself as usual.

'I'm asking you nicely. Don't make me do this the other way.'

The words were out before she could stop them. And, to her disbelief, they sounded strong, confident, forceful.

Enough that her mother bit back the retort which was on her lips.

For several long moments the two women faced off against each other. It took everything she had, but Fliss refused to back down. Not this time.

'You will regret this.'

'No.' Fliss shook her head. 'The only thing I regret is not doing this sooner.'

Perhaps then she wouldn't have lost someone as special as Ash from her life.

Ash had no idea where he was heading. He'd been driving in circles for the last two hours without seeing anything. He'd left Fliss's house intent on driving back home, sorting his kit out and leaving early for the next posting. Anything to get his mind off Fliss. But his heart had known what his head hadn't yet been ready to accept.

However hard he tried, he couldn't shake her from his head. Her desperate, ravaged face, or her defeated stance. Everything about her marked her as a different person to the Major he'd been instantly attracted to. The woman he'd fallen in love with. It killed him to see her allowing herself to be pulled down as she had tonight, but he couldn't have stayed. He'd tried to help her see the truth but she hadn't wanted to listen.

Pressing his foot on the accelerator, Ash tried to ignore the voice in the back of his head. But, however fast he drove, he wasn't going to out-run it.

The control he'd kept tonight, not for himself but for Fliss, told him how far *he* had come in less than a month. And that was down to her. If he loved her the way he claimed to, shouldn't he be prepared to fight for her? Shouldn't he try for longer than one evening, to help her to fight for herself?

And he *did* love her. He loved her intelligence, her focus, her dry sense of humour, her hidden sense of adventure, as much as he loved her lips, her body, the way she always broke apart in his arms.

Checking the road around him, Ash felt a rush of adrenalin surge through his system and it had nothing whatsoever to do with the slick, if illegal, U-turn he had just executed in the last turning lane of the dual carriageway.

By the time he got back to her house it was bathed in darkness.

CHAPTER THIRTEEN

ASH SPOTTED FLISS the instant she stepped out of the car with the General. Ash stopped dead on the field where he was supposed to be warming up with his team, his chest constricting. The inter-battalion rugby match was the last place he'd expected to see her, and he couldn't help wondering if she was sending him a message.

He watched her nervously smooth down her dress, barely even noticing the garment itself, and then, as though sensing his eyes upon her, lifted her head and looked right at him.

For a moment he thought he saw a hint of a smile but, before he could respond, a bellow pulled him up sharply.

'Heads up!'

Split second reactions served him well as he caught the well-placed throw of a teammate, pulling the ball into his gut and taking off down the field for thirty or so metres before lobbing the ball to another team-mate to do the same back up the pitch.

By the time he looked up again, Fliss was already disappearing into the marquee set up for family and friends.

He should play it cool.

Instead, he found himself yelling an excuse across the field before striding over the grounds and into the tent. He marched straight up to her, the people milling around only cranking the tension up further, making the need for formality all the more crucial.

'Major.'

'Colonel.'

'Colonel.' The deep voice of Fliss's uncle had Ash swinging around. He hadn't even noticed the old man there.

'General—' Ash greeted him as protocol demanded '—it's very good of you to take time out to attend our rugby match.'

'I hope it's going to be a good match; I want to see that trophy returned to its rightful place.'

'The lads are all geared up, sir. We fully intend to have that trophy in your hands by the end of the day.'

It was like some kind of unending torture. With no notion that Ash was actually there to talk to Fliss, the General was likely to keep the conversation pleasant for a while. It was something of a relief when the older man was pulled away by his aide-de-camp in order to greet a VIP.

He turned back to Fliss. The air between them crackled with unspoken questions. The situation was impossible. Suddenly, Ash didn't care any more.

'Walk with me,' he ordered.

'I...now?' She panicked, dropping her voice to a low tone. 'People will wonder.'

'It wasn't a request.' He didn't bother lowering his voice.

Nor did he worry about the curious eyes on them as he took her elbow and steered her out of the tent.

'Are you okay?'

She swivelled her head to look at him. 'I thought you didn't want any more to do with me?'

Ash didn't even bother to hide his disapproval. 'That isn't exactly what I said.'

'No,' she acknowledged after a moment. 'It isn't. I'm sorry, I'm just nervous. I wanted to tell you I stood up to my mother.'

Surprise swept through him, followed by the whisper of a promise.

'Why are you here?' he demanded abruptly.

Her gaze didn't waver although he could read the nerves behind those insanely blue eyes.

'Because you said you were playing in the match and I wanted to tell you. To thank you, I suppose.'

'I came to the house.'

This time it was her turn to be surprised.

'That night—' he shrugged '—all the lights were off. Your car was gone. I figured you were out.'

'I went to my uncle's...' She faltered. 'Once I'd asked my mother to leave I didn't want to stay there alone until I'd had the locks changed. Not that she'd do anything. Just... I needed the company.'

'What did your uncle say?'

'He told me that he was glad I'd finally stood up to her. He'd also like to shake *your* hand, not that he knows it was you, of course. But he wanted to thank whoever it was who finally made me see her for what she is.'

'That must have been difficult to hear,' he murmured. He could read Fliss only too well.

'Yeah—' she swallowed '—it was. But it was time. Anyway, you still haven't told me what you came back for.'

'I couldn't leave it the way I did. I had to try again. I needed to make you see what she was doing to you. Or, rather, what *you* were letting happen to you.'

'So you really came back?'

'Yes.'

He could see the pleasure in her expression

and couldn't stop himself from wanting to make it shine all the brighter.

'In the boot of my car right now is a fresh overnight bag. I thought I'd try again straight after the matches. I didn't expect to see you here.'

'I came because you said you were playing today. I wanted to see you,' she blurted out. 'I asked my uncle to bring me along as his guest; given the number of functions he's asked me to accompany him to over the years, I didn't think he'd mind.'

'I'd have thought that would arouse his suspicions.'

'Maybe.' She shrugged as though she truly didn't care. 'Especially after that little performance you put on, manhandling me back there.'

'Hardly,' he scorned before realising she was trying, in her own way, to tease him.

He wanted to know more, wanted to sort it out with her. But he forced himself to hang back. He was sure of his feelings but he needed to be sure of hers. It was testing his self-restraint to the limits. He felt as though an elastic band were pulled tight around his chest, holding a plethora of emotions in check until he knew she was ready for them. Ready for him.

He had to know what stage of their relationship—or not—she had reached. Without anything from him colouring it or pushing her along faster than she was prepared to go.

'Tell me what's in your head. This isn't going to work if you believe I said I didn't want anything more to do with you.'

Her pupils skittered from his left eye to his right eye.

'I said I was sorry about that,' she choked out.

'I know that.' He took her hands in his, both to soothe and to reassure, not even thinking about who might see them. 'I'm not asking for an apology. I'm asking you if you can trust me *now*? Can you talk to me, Fliss? Because until you feel comfortable enough to tell me, I can't help. Right now, the ball's in your court.'

'This isn't easy, you know.'

'I do know,' he vowed. 'But I can't just have part of you, Fliss. It would never be enough. I need you. Body, heart *and* mind.'

She swallowed hard but said nothing. After what seemed like an age she pulled her hands out of his, glancing around nervously. Then, dropping them to her sides, she turned away from him, walking further up the field.

Ash fell into step alongside her, forcing himself to be patient, to give her space, resisting the impulse to simply drag her into his arms and kiss her so thoroughly that she'd realise she couldn't be without him either.

But whether he won her or not, Ash finally acknowledged that he would rather have known this love with Fliss only to lose her, than the alternative. Never having had Fliss in his life, in his heart, would have been worse than any pain he might suffer now if she walked away from him.

They walked in silence. Going up the field, along the field at the top and back down to the pitches. Just when he thought it was going to all start falling down around him, she stopped as abruptly as she had started.

'I want to talk to you, Ash.' She turned to face him, an urgency in her tone. 'I came here *to* talk to you. But now that you're standing here I can't find the words to explain. Especially with practically the whole battalion and their partners wondering what we're doing out here.'

Which meant the General would be wondering what the two of them were doing out here. He hadn't thought that out properly when he'd steered Fliss by the elbow before.

'Meet me tomorrow,' he told her as he began jogging backwards, back towards his team.

'Not later?' She frowned uncertainly, but Ash couldn't help that.

'No. I've got something critical I can't afford to put off.'

And a match trophy he couldn't afford not to bring home.

CHAPTER FOURTEEN

'COLONEL, GOOD TO see you again.'

'Captain Wyland.' Ash greeted the eager young officer warmly.

'I believe I have you to thank for my appointment as ADC. So thank you, sir. It meant a lot.'

The lad had been a second lieutenant in one of Ash's units when Ash had marked him out as a potential high-flyer, and a possible aide-de-camp for a general. It was satisfying to see his instincts had been right. Not that he was about to say that to the Captain.

'You were the one who put the extra effort in, so you don't need to thank me,' Ash replied firmly. 'You worked for this promotion and you deserved it.'

'Still, thank you, Colonel.'

Ash dipped his head in concession.

'Anyway, General Delaunay is just finishing up on the phone,' the Captain apologised. 'We're running a little late, I'm afraid.'

'Right,' he offered grimly.

Just about refraining from pacing the office,

Ash considered his approach. He'd already pulled a considerable number of strings to get an audience with the General without the added complication of time constraints. He knew the man well enough on a professional basis, but turning up without an appointment to ask the General for his niece's hand in marriage was a completely different thing.

Not that it mattered—whether the older man approved or not wouldn't change Ash's feelings for Fliss. But, for her sake, he knew she'd prefer to have her uncle's blessing.

'You can go straight in now, sir.'

The Captain's voice permeated his thoughts as Ash straightened his hat, black with its red band, having swapped his usual combat attire for semi-formal dress for the meeting. Satisfied, Ash marched into the office, coming to attention in front of the General's desk, where he saluted and stayed at attention.

He hadn't done an Army meeting like this in a long time. And he hadn't met a girl's parents, *ever.* It seemed that Fliss's effect on him was more far-reaching than even he had realised. He suppressed a grin, knowing the General wouldn't be too impressed.

'Colonel Stirling, twice in as many days?' He quirked an eyebrow. 'I have to admit I was rather surprised to see your name in my diary for today. Please, take a seat.'

Removing his hat in surprise, Ash sat in the indicated chair as the General called through to his ADC, 'Captain, we'll have that coffee now, please. And you may close the door as you leave.'

Ash couldn't resist. 'Is this because we brought the trophy home yesterday, General? I'm afraid this meeting is of a more personal nature.'

'I rather thought it might be.' The General nodded. 'You're dating my niece.'

Dating? Ash thought as the Captain came back in with the coffee. That was one word for it. Still at least that was one thing he could improve on.

'I'd like to marry her.'

'I see.'

A hush blanketed the room for several minutes as both men fell silent, punctuated only by the sound of the tea being poured and the clink of the spoons against the china cups.

'Thank you.' Ash came to, taking the proffered item.

The General crossed the room again, unhurried, deliberate, picking up his own cup and returning to sit down opposite Ash.

'So, you want to marry Felicity?'

'I do.' Ash wasn't intimidated. He'd held his own enough not to worry about a general, but he did respect the man. 'I love Fliss. And I know that your blessing would mean a lot to her.'

'And I've always had you pegged as an Army man through and through.' The General's voice was careful, as though he was holding back.

Unable to put his finger on it, Ash decided not to overanalyse and instead offered a rueful shrug. '*I* always had me pegged as an Army man through and through, General. But then I met Fliss.'

'Do you think she loves you?'

Placing his cup and saucer down on the coffee table, the General rested his elbows on the arms of his chair and steepled his fingers in front of his face. A silent invitation.

With anyone else Ash might have felt riled. He might have decided to leave. But the General was a man he respected and, more than that, he was Fliss's uncle. Ash was determined to do this right.

'I know she does,' Ash answered simply.

Another moment of silence.

'I'd be inclined to agree with you.'

'Sir?'

'I heard about what happened with her mother, and that Felicity finally stood up to her. I can only assume that's in no small part down to you.'

'I just told her what I thought.'

'Indeed. And I'm grateful. But that doesn't mean I think you're the right choice for my niece.'

The words swiped Ash's legs out from under him.

'Then you're wrong,' Ash asserted calmly. 'I'm exactly the right choice for Fliss. Not some surgeon who's more interested in advancing his own career than in Fliss advancing hers.'

'Of course not,' the General scoffed. 'The man was a Muppet. But that doesn't make *you* a good match for her.'

'Is that so, General?' Cool, direct, Ash fought to control the icy fury threatening his own sanity.

'I'm sorry. I know you as a selfless, loyal, courageous soldier, an inspiring leader of men and an honourable individual. You're someone I would be proud to fight alongside. But you and I both know, Colonel, that those qualities don't necessarily translate to being a good husband, or dependable family man.'

'I would have thought they were definitely transposable,' Ash refuted steadily.

'Colonel… *Ash*…' The General softened his words, looking almost apologetic. 'You're a maverick; you're known for it. Look at the sacrifice you were prepared to make when that grenade was thrown at your men. And that's only one of many. Sometimes I feel you seem to go *seeking* the most dangerous route. So what happens when you aren't a single man any more? If you make the ultimate sacrifice and leave behind a devastated wife. Maybe even a baby one day.'

'It's called the ultimate sacrifice for a reason,' Ash pointed out, flattening his palm against his knee to stop himself from clenching his fist in frustration, his mind seeking a way to pull the conversation back. Things weren't going at all as he had envisaged.

'Then you'll understand me when I say you're exactly the kind of soldier I want as a commanding officer, but you're not the kind of husband I want for my niece. Felicity will marry you whatever I say, if that's what she wants. But, as you said before, neither of you actually need my permission, and I wouldn't dream of standing in your way. In fact, I'm happy you love each other that much. I just can't, in all good conscience, tell her I'm happy that it's an infantryman she's chosen.'

Despite his conviction, the older man sounded as though he was genuinely sorry. But still, Ash had to school himself not to react. Even though he had considered all of this himself, it was still difficult to hear.

He sucked in a breath, his chest tight.

'I *do* understand what you're saying, General. Which is why I've already applied for a transfer. Give me a role in your headquarters and I'll take myself off the front line.'

The words hung there between them, heavy and ominous. The General eyed him with concern.

'I don't think you've thought this through. I'm not trying to give you an ultimatum, Asher, I'm trying to help you. And Felicity. In the only way I know how.'

'General—' Ash cut across him '—I *have* thought this through. Ever since I realised I was in love with Fliss. I do understand why you're concerned about your niece marrying a front line soldier. We both know how close I came to the end the day that grenade was tossed through that window, and we both know what can happen in a firefight out there. We also both know that I've been offered some great postings based back home in the past, but I've never wanted to take them.'

'And now you do?' The General shook his head. 'That's commendable, Asher, it really is. But it's also naive. What happens in a year? Five years? When you miss being in the action, the adrenalin rush, the feeling of victory? However well-intentioned you are now in giving it up for Felicity, ultimately you'll start to resent what you had to give up. You'll start to resent *her*.'

'You haven't,' Ash pointed out calmly.

'Say again?'

'You were a formidable major on the front line, General. I've heard the stories about you, sir. Who hasn't? But you gave it up for Felicity, partly because she was your niece and you love her but also partly out of familial obligation.'

'And I've never once regretted that.' The General's tone changed, became short and clipped, but Ash had never been easily intimidated.

'Exactly my point. Now *I'm* prepared to give up a job I used to loved because I'm *in love* with Felicity. Not out of obligation but because I want to be with her. And not because it's a grand gesture, but because since your niece swept into my life like some kind of blonde-haired, blue-eyed tornado, I've felt more settled and content than I ever have before. Because the job I loved up until a month ago no longer holds the same draw, not since Fliss showed me a different life. So this is my way of proving to her how much she's changed me.'

'I rather think, Asher,' the General mused, 'that you have changed yourself.'

Ash suppressed a rueful smile. The more time

he spent with the General, the more he sounded like Rosie and Wilf.

'Then it's with the right person nudging me.' He smiled wryly.

'Indeed.' The General rose slowly to his feet. 'Well, I think you've made your argument very successfully, Ash.' He outstretched his hand. 'Welcome to our little family.'

'Thank you.' Ash nodded. 'Now, there's just one thing I'd like to ask you to do.'

CHAPTER FIFTEEN

'WHAT ARE WE doing here?' Fliss glanced around the Army camp as her uncle's vehicle drove slowly through the gates.

'You'll soon find out.'

Fliss snapped her head back in surprise, unaccustomed to her uncle's tone. He sounded almost...*mischievous?* It had been this way for the last hour, when he'd arrived at her home and asked her to come for a ride with him. She'd been intrigued—she was used to his commanding air, his empathetic side, and his quietly contained fury, but she couldn't remember her uncle ever having such an uncharacteristic air of mystery about him.

Slowly the four-by-four pulled over into the old FIBUA she remembered telling Ash about back in Camp Razorwire and her heartbeat began to pick up a steady rhythm.

Had he remembered?

She spun around in her seat, wondering how her uncle factored into it.

'Wait—why did you really bring me here?'

'Someone asked me to. And I liked what he had to say, so here you are. The rest, Felicity my dear, is up to you.'

An eagerness spiked low in her abdomen. The mock-up town, peppered as it was with bullet holes and crumbled sections of pretend housing, held so many fond memories for Fliss. The place had long since been abandoned by the military in favour of a bigger, newly built urban training area and now, bathed in a warm sun-set, the place almost looked beautiful with grass growing through the dusty ground and small trees sprouting up through concrete floors. Like nature reclaiming an abandoned civilisation, the cycle of life.

Her uncle's vehicle departed, slowly so as not to leave dust in its wake, and Fliss became aware of a figure walking towards her.

Ash.

Her heart felt as though it was hammering against her ribs, fervently trying to escape its cage.

'Quite a man, your uncle,' Ash said evenly as he approached. 'Even when he isn't busy being a general.'

'I can't believe you went to speak to him,' she said softly. 'And I can't believe you remembered what I told you about this place.'

'I hoped you'd like it. I'm not good at this romance thing.'

'This is perfect,' she assured him. 'This is where I trained when I was doing my medical degree. All those long hours, learning to treat casualties under fire. Learning how to be an army combat doctor. Learning the skills which had finally given me the confidence that, even if my private life—my family life—was a complete mess, then I was still skilled and infinitely competent when I came here.'

He held his arm out to her and she obliged, linking with his as she let him lead her around the old mock-town.

'This is where you put most of your past behind you and looked forward to a bright future?' Ash guessed.

His ability to read her made her feel even more comfortable and relaxed.

'Do you know I saved my first life here?'

'Tell me about it.'

'It started as a routine house-clearing training exercise. But then turned potentially fatal when one of the younger recruits become too over-eager and leapt out of the second-storey window. I ended up performing an emergency tracheotomy amongst other things.'

How long ago that felt now. But it was the moment she'd first felt like a real doctor.

'This place holds some really special memories for me,' she whispered, marvelling at how good it felt to share them with Ash and know that he understood where she was coming from.

She stopped so suddenly she jerked his arm.

'I really need to say this. Thank you, for what you said to my mother, and for what you said to me *about* her. I needed to hear that, even if I didn't exactly process it well at the time. But, most of all, thank you for what you said about me. About me deserving more and being worth more. I think I'd forgotten that.'

'You had where your mother was concerned.' He reached out to cup her jaw and her body fired into life. She barely resisted the impulse to tilt her head into his palm.

'I talked to her, you know,' Fliss told him. 'That night, I asked her all the questions which had been swirling around my head since I was a kid. I think it helped me to understand her better.'

'You need to cut her out completely, not try to understand her.'

His obvious protectiveness was touching and Fliss rose up on her tiptoes to press a quick kiss to his lips.

'I just mean that I guess, as odd as it probably sounds, in her own twisted way she thought she *was* doing something good for me by taking me from my grandparents' home with her. She hated the stifling life with its never-ending rules and boundaries. I think maybe she thought she was doing me a favour by not leaving me there.'

'That's one way to look at it.' Ash didn't look convinced but, instead of shutting herself off to him, Fliss found herself wanting to help him to understand.

'She was still a kid herself. And an immature one at that. She was wrong to make me responsible for her happiness when her own dreams died, but she wasn't the only one at fault. My grandparents weren't exactly perfect themselves.

'I grew up feeling culpable and worthless, and all the other cruel jibes she threw at me on a daily basis. And it went on for so long that even when my uncle tracked us down and took me home I realised that most of what she had told me was right. My grandparents took me in because they felt it was their duty. They were obliged to care for their daughter's fatherless child.'

Ash frowned at her.

'I thought you loved your life once your uncle took you home? I thought he saved you.'

'He did—he was fantastic,' Fliss cried, panicking that she might be portraying her incredible uncle—her rock—in anything other than glowing terms when she thought of all he had done for her. 'He has always been fantastic.'

'But your grandparents weren't?'

She drew in a deep breath, unsure how to explain this to a man who had been physically hurt and wounded as a child.

'They were never unkind to me,' she said slowly. 'They gave me a home, schooling, clothing, everything a child needs physically. But they never showed me any love. My uncle was away a lot with the Army so it was usually just me with them. I worked hard; my grades were outstanding because I thought it was about their fear of me making the same mistakes as my mother. I thought if I worked hard I could show them that I wasn't like that, that I would earn their love.'

'But it didn't work,' he guessed.

She supposed he knew enough about that. If the love wasn't there naturally from the start, then she was hardly going to earn it.

'No,' she confirmed. 'It didn't. I suppose it turned out for all of us to be my way of repaying them for taking me in. My success was confirmation they were meeting my needs. But it didn't change who I was or what I was. Behind the perfunctory *well done*s they never stopped looking at me as the family's shameful little secret.'

Raking his hand over his forehead, Ash closed the gap between them but he still wasn't touching her. She inhaled deeply, the familiar scent both soothing her troubled mind and stimulating her body.

Oh, so stimulating.

'I don't want to talk about it any more,' she said gently. 'I've told you now. And it's done and it's my past. *All* of it.'

She licked her lips, hoping she hadn't misread the signals.

'So how about we focus on the future? One with both of us in it?' She hesitated for a moment. 'You told me you loved me. There is still an *us*, isn't there?'

He'd told her he loved her, but that was before. She had no idea if he still felt the same way.

'Is it really what you want?' He stepped forward, his fingers lacing through hers. He tipped his forehead against hers until she thought the pressure in her chest would compact her.

'Are you all in, Fliss?'

'I'm all in,' she murmured. 'You changed everything for me. You make me feel stronger than I've ever felt. More sure of who I am and what I want. And you give me a sense of belonging.'

Lifting her hands to his mouth, Ash dropped kisses on her knuckles.

'Want to see something incredible?'

She barely hesitated before accepting his hand, allowing him to lead her in companionable silence through the FIBUA towards where, now she was looking, a faint glow appeared to be coming from one of the rooftops. She shivered with anticipation, and it was nothing to do with the cooling evening air. Still, she was glad of the trainers and warm jumper her uncle had told her to wear.

'You know, I don't know whether to be impressed or concerned at the thought of you and my uncle conspiring against me.'

'Whichever you prefer.'

She could hear the smile in his voice.

Together, they made their way past the deserted buildings until the source of the glow became more apparent. She detected the woody scent of a burn, tasting it faintly on the air even before the flickering firelight spilled from the roof of the building in front of her. The crackle of it carried in the still air, making it feel romantic, Fliss thought as they crossed the road and headed up the stone steps which led to the roof.

Her breath lodged in her throat like a tiny bird fluttering its wings, unable to get out of its cage. The old concrete roof was covered with a large rug, a picnic basket and two fold-out chairs on top. A fire pit threw out heat from the front whilst military glow sticks lined the three sides of the perimeter like an Army version of fairy lights. For an instant it evoked memories of being on the viewing point with Ash when they'd watched the carnival floats and something twisted inside Fliss. Hot, red, sensual.

But it was only when she turned around that the full extent of Ash's military make-over became apparent. The fourth perimeter wall which formed the back of the building was two metres high and—right now—it was covered in a mural. The most stunning graffiti art Fliss had ever seen and there was no doubt that it was a faithful representation of the view from the rooftop of the MERT compound back at Camp Razorwire.

'It's stunning,' she breathed, spinning slowly to look at Ash. 'But how…?'

'You remember Corporal Hollings? Andy Hollings?' Ash prompted.

How could she forget the soldier she and Ash had first worked together to save? The reason Ash had come up onto that rooftop back at camp, to tell her the lad had been deemed stable enough to fly back to hospital in the UK.

'Of course I remember.'

'Well, his brother does this for a living; commercial businesses and local councils commission him to paint the gable walls of buildings, under bridge arches—you name it.'

'How do you know that?' She shook her head incredulously.

'He had an unusual tattoo so I asked him about it during that period where he was slipping in and out and you were trying to keep him awake.'

Fliss nodded slowly. 'I remember, but I never heard what he said.'

'He told me it was based on his brother's first piece of work. When I thought about doing this for you—for us—I thought it would be a nice touch. I had a photo from that rooftop so...'

He shrugged, tailing off, but Fliss was still waiting for her heart to start beating.

'So there is an *us*?' The grin spread through her body like warm honey.

Smiling, Ash led her to the chairs, helping her sit down in one whilst he sat in the other; they leaned into each other, his fingers still laced with hers. She didn't even bother trying to drag her eyes from his until he answered.

'There is, without a doubt, an *us*.'

The heat of the fire was much more apparent here but Fliss suspected it wasn't what was causing the warmth to seep through her body, through her very bones, right now.

'You're strong, Fliss. And you're driven. You

have so many incredible qualities, from your empathy and loyalty to your passion and dedication. And I have to tell you, you're damn sexy too. You affect me in a way I can't control.'

'I'm glad,' she murmured.

'And I love that about you.'

The words slid through her. So subtly she wasn't sure if she was hearing things.

'You still love me?'

She swallowed. Hard. It seemed almost too perfect. Too unreal.

'I love everything about you, Fliss. You turn my heart inside out.'

'I do?' she breathed, marvelling at the man facing her. The same one she'd challenged in that office, in the supply room, in the hotel room. And yet a completely different, more open person.

But only open to her, which somehow made it all the more incredible.

'I love the doctor you are, Fliss, I love the Major you are, and the person you are. Most of all I love the woman you are. The way you make *me* want to be a better soldier, better leader, better person. I love the way you make me feel, the way you get under my skin like no one else, the way you challenge me and don't let up. And, for the record, I love the sexy way you bite your lip like that.'

'You love me,' Fliss repeated, the confusion of emotions that had been jostling in her brain finally settling down enough for her to understand his declaration.

It was more than she had dreamed of. A passionate, heartfelt, amazing declaration of love she had never thought anyone would ever say to her. It made her feel part of something special. It made her feel they were something special. Not practical, logical, or sensible. But unrestrained, emotional, intense.

'I love you too.' She stumbled over the words in her haste to say them. To hear what they sounded like when accompanied with all these sensations tumbling around her heart.

They sounded magical. Unparalleled. Perfect.

The feeling started in her curling toes and permeated up through her legs, her body, her chest, fixing an outrageous grin on her mouth as it continued right up to the top of her head. She felt as though together they could face anything.

Together.

She started as Ash slid off his chair in front of her, simultaneously retrieving a neat green leather box from beneath her fold-out chair.

'Marry me, Major.' He grinned. 'It isn't practical or logical but I don't want to do the practical thing and wait until we've dated for a while, because it won't change anything. No other woman could match you. No other woman could affect me the way you do. There will never be another one for me. So I don't want us to wait.'

Fliss could scarcely breathe. It was as though he'd read every last emotion written in her heart and he was rewriting her future even as he did so, throwing out her old rulebook and giving her more freedom. A future with Ash sparkled in a way she'd never dreamed possible.

'I don't want to wait either,' she breathed as he slid the ring onto her finger, then cupped her jaw and drew her into the sweetest yet most intense kiss.

It seemed to last an eternity, drawing her down into its aching longing and beauty. She wrapped her arms around Ash's neck and held herself as close to his body as she could, as if to convince herself that it truly was real and not one of those bubbles about to pop any moment.

By the time they eventually came up for air, Fliss felt more at peace with herself than she ever had.

A sliver of mischief slipped into her head. Sliding off the chair, she pushed Ash's shoulders until he was on his back on the rug, then she moved astride him.

'What, exactly, are you doing?' Ash demanded, the cocked eyebrow suggesting he knew exactly what was on her mind.

Leaning forward, she dropped a kiss to his lips as she shushed him.

'Last time we were outdoors like this, back at the carnival, you taught me something I'd never done before. But when I tried to do something for you, you wouldn't relinquish the reins.' Reaching down, she began to unbuckle his belt, thrilling in the sensation of him finally allowing her to take control.

'I think it's time I repaid that favour.'

His body, already hard against hers, now reacted even further under her touch, making Fliss feel more powerful than ever before.

'Fine,' he managed through gritted teeth. 'But, just so you know, I intend us to spend a lifetime learning new things about each other. And for us to repay each other so many favours that we lose track of whose turn it is, and we won't even care.'

'I can't wait,' Fliss managed, as Ash shifted deliberately beneath her.

And then she resumed her own task, feeling him give himself up to her the way she always did for him. The way she would for him later that night. The way she knew they both would for the rest of their lives.

Because sometimes it was good to lose control.

* * * * *

If you enjoyed this story, check out these other great reads from Charlotte Hawkes

**THE SURGEON'S BABY SURPRISE
THE ARMY DOC'S SECRET WIFE**

Available now!